Derrin's
Hot Pursuit

Tucker Davis

Derrin's Hot Pursuit

A Chasing Love Novel

Outskirts Press, Inc.
Denver, Colorado

Derrin's Hot Pursuit
A Chasing Love Novel

Outskirts Press, Inc.
http://www.outskirtspress.com

ISBN: 978-1-4327-8236-8

Outskirts Press and the "OP" logo are trademarks belonging to Outskirts Press, Inc.

PRINTED IN THE UNITED STATES OF AMERICA

ACKNOWLEDGEMENTS

First and foremost, thanks to my heavenly Father, without whom I could not have realized this dream come true. I must thank my husband, Anthony for his patience when I stayed up late writing. A special thanks to my children, Dallas and Ashley who are learning the importance of having a voice.

Many thanks to all my family, friends, fans and supporters, without you I would not be able to continue. A special thanks to my Hair Sculpture unofficial book club: You guys are the soil from which my ideas grow.

I'd like to thank two people who assisted me in moving my vision for this novel from my mind to reality. First, thank you to Jodee Thayer, my publishing consultant, without her insight and direction the novel would not have had its polished look and feel. Next, I must thank Michael Botelho who molded my cover image, font style and summary into a beautiful work of art.

I hope you enjoy Chloe and Derrin's love affair. Happy reading!

PROLOGUE

Derrin reached over to the passenger seat of his BMW 750 and picked up two folders and pushed aside current copies of USA Today, the Wall Street Journal and the Atlanta Journal Constitution. He figured he would need all the reading materials he could get as he waited for Chloe to return home. He had been sitting in her driveway for a few sporadic hours at a time all week, but unfortunately she had yet to make an appearance.

Today he figured he might as well wait her out because there was no way he was going into another weekend without holding her, kissing her until he got his fill, or inhaling and tasting her until she moaned his name. He realized Chloe was upset with him and had sent word to him to leave her alone. But he was not one to take orders from anyone and he definitely was not going to take orders from her gold digging friend Cara or her man hating cousin Diane.

After leaving her a voicemail every hour on the hour for the last four days, he decided to take matters into his own hands. He was going to talk to her once and for all, if he could only get her to come home. Derrin glanced at his watch and it was almost six o'clock in the evening. Chloe usually got off work at 5:30 unless she had a special project to finish. Maybe that was the reason she was not home all week. She was working on a special project. But why hadn't she returned his calls or answered her cell phone. No, she was avoiding him. He just knew it. So here he was sitting in his new black BMW admiring the caramel leather seats and recalling how Chloe looked sitting beside him when he took her out.

Chloe, unlike the other women he dated or bedded, was different. Yes, he could not believe at twenty-six she was still a virgin. Well, at least she was until she walked into the guest bedroom at his fraternity brother's house and laid down beside him. At the thought of what transpired, Derrin smiled.

CHAPTER ONE

FIVE MONTHS EARLIER.

Chloe had come in the bedroom to escape the party scene. She claimed to have had a migraine headache and just needed to lie down. But the B.C. powder and Coca-Cola she gulped down took its toll very quickly and she could hardly keep her eyes open. She fell on the bed and was sleep before her head hit the pillow. Unknown to her, Derrin was already sleeping in the king sized bed exhausted from jet lag coupled with too many shots of Patron.

Chloe obviously was dreaming about something erotic because she moaned in her sleep. Her breathy moans caused something in Derrin to react and he inched closer to her with each sound. He felt as though he was being called by something out of his control. He believed he was dreaming and decided to just go with it and see where the dream took him. It took him right up behind Chloe in the bed. As the front of his thigh brushed up against her round firm, yet soft butt, he threw his leg over her as she slept on her side. The weight of his leg and the slight touch of his manhood against the middle of her butt made Chloe groan with heated expectation. She naturally scooted back against him. The softness of her butt was a trigger for his hand to caress and stroke her breasts. The more he touched her, the more intense her moans became.

Derrin, being the woman loving player he was, went into autopilot. He lay sleep and unaware of his body's reaction and interaction with Chloe Dancy. The lime green v-neck chiffon shirt she wore allowed his large chocolate brown hands easy access to her bra. With only a flick of his wrist, he had unclasped her bra and was caressing her nipples until they were perky buds waiting to be tasted. Chloe moaned and unknowingly pleaded for him to satisfy her.

His subconscious mind attempted to let him know this was no dream, but he ignored it. As he continued to caress her breasts, she turned to face him. The soft scent of her perfume and the aroused scent of her sexual readiness began to torture his senses. He licked his lips and inched his head closer to her face. Within seconds his lips were pressed against her ears. He nibbled on them and they tasted like kiwi. He loved kiwi.

The moistness of his lips and tongue caused her to pull his face, and ultimately his lips, toward her mouth. Then it happened, their lips touched and their tongues began a sensual mating dance. She tasted like peppermint. He could not get enough. His hot tongue glided over her tongue. He nipped at her lips. He continued the oral assault on her mouth until she threw her head back and sighed. She was near climax from his kiss.

He rolled over on top of her and eased his hand up her mini skirt. *No panties, pay dirt.* He subconsciously thought. His hands moved slightly across her thighs and then slowly and gently pressed against the core of her womanhood. She was hot, soft and wet. His erection grew with each touch. Derrin whispered in her ear, "Open for me baby." He softly cooed in her ear.

She responded without hesitation. His fingers stroked her womanly folds, first with swirls then with flicks. Chloe was beyond hot and bothered now. She threw her legs open like a butterfly and begged, "Please. Now."

Even a sleep and drunken Derrin could not deny a woman's pleas for satisfaction. As he began kissing her again, he pushed back from her, unzipped his pants, and freed his manhood. Sensing the presence of his manhood, Chloe softly moved the tips of her fingers from the base to the head.

She smiled in her sedated state.

Derrin slowly pressed his manhood at the entrance of her heavenly gate. She mumbled pleas for satisfaction. He eased inside her. *Hmm, what's that,* he thought. He figured he did not have the strength he normally did since this was a dream. With a little more pressure he entered her. Her moans sounded like a cry. He halted his movement and lay still. Something was wrong. Then her body began to meld to him and grip him with the pull of a plunger.

Then it happened. She opened her eyes and saw him lying on top of her. She could not see his face, but in her dreams it was always Derrin. This dream should not be an exception. She slowly opened her eyes but something told her not to scream and risk scaring him off.

Who is this man with creamy brown skin, dark low cut curly hair lying on top of me? No, lying inside of me. Chloe adjusted her head to try to get a better glimpse of his face. Then his identity became evident. She knew his every feature even without seeing his eyes. *Derrin.*

"Oh, my goodness!" Chloe gasped and jerked up.

This action snapped Derrin out of his slumber and caused his eyes to fly open. He appraised the situation and lightheartedly responded.

"Hello" he said and grinned. Then he asked, "Don't I know you?"

"I would hope so since you are buried deep within my body." Chloe said as she held onto his shoulders. Slightly encouraging him to remain right there.

"What?" He asked confused and still a little groggy. Then he realized he was having sex with a friend of his sister. He went to move and Chloe clamped her inner muscles silently letting him know she did not want him to pull out.

"Uh, I need to get up, don't you think?" Derrin softly teased.

Swallowing all her fears and attempting to sound wonton, Chloe responded.

"I thought you were a lady pleaser, Derrin. While, I don't know how we ended up in this compromising position, I would hope you would finish what you started." Then she grinned. "Or is that asking too much of you, Derrin?"

"You know I aim to please." He was proud of his reputation. Then he slowly pulled his manhood out but ever so slightly leaving the head in. His thrusts began slowly and gently, but the more he moved, the more she milked him. She closed her eyes and rotated her hips to meet his movements. This was the first time she had felt these inner muscles move. She loved the pleasure each movement he made evoked. She tried to bite her bottom lip to catch the moans. She knew she was going to have a swollen lip when this was over. But she did not care. Derrin saw her biting her lip and felt the slow trembling of her thighs. He reached under her and pulled her butt up closer to him. He was working hard to maintain his control but she was milking him like no one had ever done before. For Derrin that was saying a lot. He grunted and grumbled incoherently in her ear. He thrust harder, deeper. He could feel the muscles in his legs and stomach contract.

Chloe could not prevent the moan, or the groan, but before she could react she felt extreme pleasure erupt from her body. She had her eyes closed but she could swear everything turned white. She was shaking and trembling and breathing like she ran a marathon. So this was sex. No, she thought, this was sex with Derrin. Once he felt her release, he thrust hard twice more and his pleasure came down on him.

He rolled off her and placed his right arm over his face. He did not want his sister's friend to see his face as he felt the aftershocks of a climax. A wonderful climax.

Then it dawned on him. *Was she a virgin? No way a virgin could evoke this much pleasure. Maybe the virginal state was just a part of the dream.* He tried to figure out a way to broach the subject without offending her. He did not have to think long because Chloe lifted her torso off the bed on her elbows and turned to him.

"Thank you for my first orgasm. I owe you one." She said teasingly and fell back on the bed.

"You mean your first everything don't you?" Derrin attempted to sound blasé when he made the comment. But he moved his arm slightly to see Chloe's reaction.

She laughed and the bed slightly vibrated then she responded. "We can conquer a few more firsts, if you're game?" She said half joking and half serious. She had a few positions she'd read about and wanted to try.

"You're kidding me, right? You need to soak in a tub or something. He eased up and stood by the bed, deciding that standing would be best since he did not want to give her the impression that he was a jerk for lying next to her chastising her. Derrin always made sure all the women he dated or bedded knew the deal before he slept with them. If they did not want to accept the terms then he would keep moving on the next one. He had been burned once by love and was not ready to jump back in the fire just yet. As a result, he lived by the motto: One and done. There would be no all night phone calls, no attendance at family functions, no cuddling and no sleepovers. Chloe began talking and he was again aware of her presence.

"Oh, well. I thought one and done meant one night not one time. It's cool, though. You did your thing and I am happy as a lark." She sat up on the bed and looked down at her chest. She clasped her bra, tucked her left breast tightly in and buttoned up her shirt. The entire action was causing Derrin's mouth to water. He regretted that he never got to actually taste her soft honey colored mounds. He wondered if they tasted as good as they looked or felt. *Probably better.* Derrin tried to will himself to move his gaze from watching her hands. But he lacked the will power. He did however stop the drool from leaving his lips by pulling his bottom lip under his upper teeth. He shook his head trying to process everything.

"Who are you and what did you do with my sister's best friend? You must be a body snatcher because the Chloe I know never would randomly sleep with someone." His voice was raspy and deep, as he softly spoke.

Chloe looked up at him and met his gaze. One lone spiral curl fell into her face. She let it stay there partially covering her right eye.

His gathered eyebrows evidenced his thoughts. He seemed perplexed by her appreciation of his one and done motto and pleasure in their random sexual interaction. If only he knew, she had longed for this day ever since the first time she met him. She compared every man she met afterwards to him.

She had come to the party with her friend Cara hoping she would finally become brazen and bold enough to approach him. Cara persuaded her to take her panties off and throw them in her purse. Cara also convinced Chloe that if she felt brazen she would act brazen. Chloe realized that was part of reason she had the headache. She was overwhelmed by all the men trying to get her number or entertain her with idle chatter tonight. She wanted to star gaze after Derrin but he was nowhere to be found. Since she did not drive to the party and Cara was not ready to leave, she resorted to self-help in the form of a B.C. headache powder and a Coca-Cola.

"Chloe." Derrin's masculine voice brought her out of her trance. She looked at him.

"Chloe, I was sleeping earlier. I, uh, I did not intentionally nor purposefully set out to seduce you. I thought I was dreaming not realizing I was acting out my dreams. I would have never done this." He put his hands in his pockets and looked down at her fingers while she smoothed her shirt over her legs. His erection was growing rapidly and he tried to think of running water in order to calm down. It was not working. Luckily for him, Chloe did not notice. She was too busy fighting the urge to cry. No, ball her eyes out. Chloe jumped up from the bed trying to fight the tears.

She thought to herself. *He did not even want to sleep with me. He regrets it.*

"Derrin, I have to go. Sorry to ruin your image of me and I am definitely sorry you regret what happened." She swiftly walked to the door nearly running into the edge of the bed. Derrin attempted to reach out and grab her arm, but her movements caught him off guard and he was not quick enough. She was gone as evidenced by the emptiness he felt in the room.

He grabbed the door and instantly moved out of the room. The cool air made him glance down. His shirt was unbuttoned and his fly was open with his erection peeking out and saying hi to the world. He returned to the room and closed the door before anyone noticed him. He sure hoped he succeeded. He leaned against the back of the door. *Damn.* He wanted to chase after Chloe, but he was never one to run behind a woman not, even one who had rocked his world.

CHAPTER TWO

Over the next two weeks, Derrin could not stop dreaming about Chloe. He was becoming sleep deprived. He figured that sleeping in a bed merely reminded him of his lovemaking escapade with Chloe. He tried to sleep on the sofa, in a chair and even on the floor. Nothing worked. So, here he was begging his younger sister, Kenya to help him.

He just needed to know how to get a woman out of your mind. Once he removed Chloe from his dreams he could sleep and move on with his life. He had a good life indeed. He was a successful owner of an internet café and coffee shop in the new live-work-play community in the heart of Alpharetta, a small city north of Atlanta, Georgia. He owned a penthouse condominium at the Brookshire Lofts. He was independently wealthy, thanks to investing in the stock market before it crashed and having the forethought to cash out before it tanked. However, you could not tell his financial status by his clothes or car. He seemed to be an average Joe.

Derrin had his pick of the most beautiful women in the metro Atlanta area. Every lady he bedded knew his disclaimer of a no strings attached temporary fling. Each freely accepted the deal for a night, week or month with Derrin Reynolds. A no strings attached temporary fling was just the way he liked it. Or at least he used to like it. Since he slept with Chloe two weeks ago, he couldn't get aroused for any other woman. He had no desire to return their calls or sweet talk them out of their panties.

"No, Derrin. I am not Dear Abby or Dr. Phil." Kenya firmly said as she poured milk into a cereal bowl and grabbed her iPhone from the holster. Her voice snapped Derrin out of his thoughts.

"Come on, Sis. I really need to talk to you. I need some female advice. You wouldn't turn away your own brother would you?" Derrin sat on the bar stool in their parents' newly remodeled kitchen. His bare feet were planted on the maple hardwood floors. He batted his eyes and tried to make a sad face.

"I'm not buying it. So stop with the puppy dog impressions." Kenya did not look up from her iPhone.

"Well, I guess I will have to resort to scare tactics." Derrin paused for dramatic effect. "Either you help me or I tell Dad you spent your monthly trust check on a down payment on your ex-boyfriend's apartment. Maybe I will refer to him as your unemployed, cheating and freeloading boyfriend. Which one do you think he will like more?" Kenya looked up at him with her finger frozen mid-air over the buttons on the phone. She had fire in her eyes.

Derrin knew his sister was probably going to throw something at him, so he evaluated the objects close by before he made his declaration. He could tell by the look in her eyes and the faint red tint to her oval face that she was going to kill him. He did not care because if he did not get some sleep he was going to kill himself.

"You wouldn't dare!" Kenya put the phone down and walked toward Derrin. Derrin attempted to move from the bar stool before she got to him but once again he was too slow. Kenya kicked the leg on the stool and he went tumbling to the floor. Derrin rolled over and crawled to a standing position. His sister charged at him and he grabbed her hands and twisted them around her body. He was standing behind holding her overlapped arms, partially bent over laughing. Kenya was mad as a snake. But she could not get free.

"What's all that noise in there? Are you two okay?" Their father yelled from the living room where he was sitting in his favorite recliner watching CSI reruns.

Derrin cleared his throat and began in a slightly elevated voice, "Dad, I was meaning to tell you something." Kenya stepped on Derrin's bare foot and he screamed.

"Okay, okay. I will help you. But you better not say one more word to Dad." Derrin inwardly chuckled. This game always worked with his younger sister. She was a spoiled brat and their Dad gave her whatever she wanted but their Dad knew he had to give her monthly allowances in small portions or she would spend it needlessly. Their father had no idea that Kenya was often time supporting her no good boyfriends while they discovered themselves.

"Now, I am going to let you go. But if you hit me all bets are off."

"Alright, deal." Kenya said before Derrin slowly released her hands and then ran to the door closest to the living room. Kenya rolled her eyes and returned to her cereal.

"Can you repeat the question? I seem to have forgotten it during all the blackmailing that was going on a few minutes ago."

Derrin knew good and well that Kenya had not forgotten the question. In fact, she could probably recite the entire conversation verbatim without hesitation or thought.

"How can you get an ex-lover out of your dreams?"

Kenya, without lifting her eyes from her iPhone, frowned her face up.

"Well, first I need to know what the ex-lover is doing in the dreams and why you don't like it."

Derrin thought about how much he should tell her since Chloe had been Kenya's friend since they were roommates in their freshman year in college, nearly eight years ago.

"Let's just say this lady friend of mine is meeting my every need in my dreams. Her smile lifts me up in more ways than one, if you know what I mean." Derrin had to catch the frog in his throat. *My lady friend?*

"Why do you want her to stop? Is this person someone who you wanted to continue a relationship with after your one and done is over? Or is she someone who you couldn't satisfy so you want the dream to stop?" Kenya asked the last question out of spite.

"You know me better than that. I please all the women I sex." Kenya simply rolled her eyes and put her bowl in the sink.

She returned to the bar and placed her hands on the counter and studied her brother. He was leaving something out and she wondered what could have him all in knots. She tilted her head.

"Spill it."

"Spill what?" Derrin tried to avoid eye contact with Kenya for fear he would get loose lips.

"You know what. There is something you are not telling me about this lady in your dream. I can't help you if you don't tell me everything." Derrin glanced out the window. The sky was a clear powder blue and the clouds appeared white and fluffy, a beautiful day to upset his sister. He inhaled deeply and then began to tell Kenya what happened with Chloe.

"O-M-G! I am going to kill you for real now. How could you sleep with my friend?"

"I did not know I was sleeping with her until she nearly screamed and woke me up. I was drunk and jet lagged. Didn't you hear that part of the story?" Derrin tried to convince Kenya that it was not his fault.

"She has been in love with you ever since you moved my trunk into our dorm room freshman year. How could you?"

"Now, it's my turn to use text language – W-T-H for What the Hell?" The frantic look on Derrin's face made Kenya giggle. Her giggle turned into a full blown laugh. She bent over and grabbed her stomach. Then she picked up her iPhone and pressed a few keys.

Derrin felt the sudden urge to beg. "Ken, please don't send her a text. Let this be our little secret. If you help me this time I will get your ex-boyfriend to return the nude photos of you he is using to blackmail you into giving him money."

Kenya's eyebrows lifted nearly to the top of her forehead.
"You knew?" She dryly asked.
His Blackberry beeped. He looked down to see that he had a text.
He clicked and saw it was from Kenya and read, ROTFLMAO. He
grinned because he knew this was text language for Rolling on the
Floor Laughing My Ass Off. But when he looked back at Kenya she
had tears running down her face.
"Don't worry Kenya. I was already taking care of his sorry ass
anyway. I got the photos and negatives from him last night when I
made a surprise visit to his new apartment. He nearly died when I
punched him in the face and stepped on his hand. But he gave up the
photos. That was when I learned what he was holding over your head.
I was just trying to get him to leave you alone and stop using you. He
assumed you told me about the photos and gave them up to save his
fingers." Derrin put his hands in his pockets and slowly rocked on the
heels of his feet.
Kenya came charging at him. At first he thought she was going
to make good on her promise to kill him, but then when her arms flew
around his neck and she squeezed him with all her might, he knew she
was just expressing her gratitude.
"Thank you, thank you, and thank you!" Kenya exclaimed.
"No problem that's what big brothers are for. I burned the photos
and the negatives. You were having a bad hair day, so I thought you
would want me to destroy them." He casually shrugged.
Kenya smiled and kissed him on the cheek. "Now, I am seriously
indebted to you. Sit down and let's figure this thing with Chloe out."
They walked to the bar and talked for nearly two hours. Derrin left
his parent's house with a better understanding of women. He could
not believe that with as many women as he had been in contact with
he did not have a clue how they processed information. According
to Kenya, he needed to apologize to Chloe for making her think he
regretted their intimate encounter. Kenya said a woman like Chloe

would probably take his statements to mean he regretted the entire encounter. If she only knew how far her assessment was from the truth, she would know how wrong she was. He left believing that once he apologized to Chloe he would be able to sleep like a baby.

A baby, oh my goodness. We did not use protection. This is turning into a nightmare.

Derrin clicked his automatic garage door opener and slowly pulled into his assigned parking space. He left Kenya with a plan to go to Chloe's house, apologize, and get his life back. But what if she was pregnant with his child? He needed to call Kenya back.

"You idiot. This little revelation of yours does not change anything. You need to buy some flowers, go to Chloe's house, and do not mention anything about a baby."

"Why not? I want to know. Hell, I need to know." Derrin was getting a headache. No, more like a body ache.

"Derrin, there are so many if's that it is best if you leave the baby inquiries alone for at least another three weeks."

"Three weeks! Are you kidding me? I will be dead from worry by then."

"You big brat. Chill. Derrin, just do as I tell you. This will free your mind for sleep or at least to dream about other women you bed instead of wed. Now, good night. I need my rest."

Before he could respond, Kenya had clicked the button to end the call. He knew she did not need any rest. She was like an owl. She just did not want to talk to him anymore today.

Derrin mixed himself a drink, Crown Royal Black and cranberry juice to be exact. He gulped it down and went to his bedroom. He was determined to get some sleep tonight even if he had to get drunk to do it.

Derrin's dreams were not as vivid as usual. He could see a beautiful lady playfully running on the beach. She was laughing. Just as she was turning her head toward him something caught her attention and she ran away. Tonight he could not see her face. He watched as her white chambray shirt blew in the wind. She was moving in a slow skip. He wanted to call out to her. But he noticed she was running toward a baby. The baby's cries filled the afternoon air. Derrin thought, will someone please pick that baby up. There was no relief; all he heard were the wails of an infant. Even though he was sound asleep, he tossed and turned trying to escape the crying. Derrin finally jerked his head off the pillow and glanced at the clock. It was 5:00 a.m. At least he slept for nearly eight hours.

CHAPTER THREE

Derrin usually ran three miles before he opened the café. But this morning he was lost in his thoughts and did not realize he ran nearly four miles without stopping. He was torturing his body. He did not care. He was trying to steer clear of thoughts about Chloe and the possibility that she was pregnant with his child. Once he reached the four mile mark, he decided he had done enough running for the day.

He returned home, showered and left for the café, a mere two block walk from his condominium. He usually chanted a mantra from the 80's Dunkin Donuts television commercial, *Time to make the doughnuts. Gotta make the doughnuts.* It always made him smile and think of his childhood. However, this morning he was in a melancholy mood. He just hummed a few Kanye West songs and briskly walked to his café. The morning air was as crisp as his white linen button down shirt and as comfortable as his slightly worn denim jeans.

He arrived and was greeted by Ms. Kaye, his oldest employee. At fifty-seven, Kaye was old in age but she was spry and young as the twenty year olds. Kaye claimed working around so many young people kept her young.

"Good morning, young buck. How are things today?" Ms. Kaye was filling the sugar containers to place on the tables.

"It's morning not sure if it is good though." Derrin moved past Ms. Kaye and pushed open the double wide swing doors leading to the kitchen. He needed coffee. He did not care for a latte or cappuccino today. He wanted black coffee with no sugar and no cream. He moved around the kitchen with the grace of a swan. After the coffee was set to start brewing, he pulled out a newspaper from his backpack and placed it on the counter.

Ms. Kaye entered the kitchen and barely glanced his way. He knew she was just waiting to find the proper time or words to ask him what was bothering him. He tried to pretend he was engrossed in the news.

She cleared her throat and began.

"You know, women are simple creatures. Even though you men claim you don't understand us or that we are from Mars or Venus. I can't remember which planet we are supposed to be from. But, we are simple creatures. All you need to do is take the time to listen to our words and our hearts." She picked up a large plastic bag of napkins and began walking back toward the exit.

Derrin did not want to be disrespectful, but he definitely disagreed with her proclamation.

"It's not as straightforward as you believe, Ms. Kaye. Women may be simple but their desires are not. They say they want one thing but in reality they really want another. Consequently, it's best to keep them all at arm's length." Derrin blew out a soft burst of air from his lungs and turned the page of the newspaper.

Ms. Kaye chuckled and batted her right hand at him. She turned around just before she was fully out of the room.

"Like I said you need to listen to our words and hearts. They never lie. Your problem is you are just trying to hear what you want to hear." She left him to consider her words.

Derrin pondered her words and thought to himself. *She is just old. She does not know what she is talking about. Women are teasers who say they want the white picket fence, two and half children, a dog and a mini-van, when really they want to break your heart in a million pieces after you give them what they say they want. Humph.*

His Blackberry began vibrating in his front pants pocket. He looked at it and saw it was his sister, Kenya. Derrin was feeling a headache coming on.

"Hello. What's up Ken?"

"Nothing. I was calling to see if you have mapped out a plan to see Chloe. I think you really need to get it over with as soon as possible. Kenya was practically smiling through the phone. The pitch of her voice revealed she had an ulterior motive.

"I don't have a plan Kenya. I am going to have a bouquet of flowers delivered with a note attached. End of story." Derrin huffed into the phone and reared back on the legs of the chair.

"Okay, but you will never get her out of your dreams that way."

"Sure I will. In fact, I had a drink last night and slept until morning. She is already on the way out of my dreams." He did not want to tell her that he dreamed about a woman and a baby for fear that she would go overboard.

"I am going to say this one time and one time only. Go get the flowers from the florist. Yellow roses to be exact. Hand deliver them to her yourself and give your apology in person not written on some card. She may surprise you and forgive you for your arrogance."

"I'll think about it. I have to get work, we open in an hour. Love you." Derrin disconnected the call and put his hands behind his head. He reasoned that it would not hurt if he delivered the flowers in person. It was the least he could do after he caused her to run away from him crying.

The remainder of the day was uneventful. Derrin chatted with his regular customers and flirted with several female customers. He was quite pleased that his spirits lifted after his rocky start. It was probably due to the call from Kenya or perhaps his decision to follow her advice.

It was nearly 6:00 p.m. and it was time for him to go make the bank deposit and leave for the day. His night manager was more than capable to handle things. After he left the bank, he went to a florist inside the local grocery store. He picked a bouquet that was a mix of yellow roses, pink carnations and tiny white tulips. He thought they were pretty. He only hoped Chloe did too.

He returned to his car and placed the bouquet on the front passenger seat. Derrin did not know the exact address but he knew how to get to Chloe's house. So he turned off his GPS navigation system and made his way up to Duluth. After a few wrong turns, he finally found the street that he believed Chloe lived on. He had dropped Kenya off several times in the past six months, but at the time he was preoccupied with getting to his next stop to take note of any particulars about the neighborhood. Now, he took note of the aesthetic quality of the neighborhood. The houses were set back from the street but not so far that the neighbors could not see when you had company. The landscaping and side yards contributed to the impression that the homes were custom built. They were all mainly two level homes, a few with front porches and others with side entrances and three car garages. *What does she do again?* Derrin asked himself.

He found the street number of the house that was in the text he got from Kenya. He slowly eased into the driveway. Lucky for him her front door was on the side of her house and the driveway was partially shielded by the hedges. He sat in the car for a few minutes to gather his thoughts. *This will be easy. Say hello, apologize and get the hell out of here.* Derrin had no idea why he was so nervous about seeing Chloe again. He wiped the moisture from his palms, grabbed the flowers and exited the car.

CHAPTER FOUR

From the front entrance he could hear a woman singing and soft music playing. *Does she have company? I hope not. Should I come back?* After much mental debate, Derrin pressed the doorbell.

Chloe had just changed clothes from her shower. Her hair was damp in the back along her neck so she pinned it up to the top of her head. She usually slept in a fitted t-shirt and panties. But tonight she pulled on some red sweatpants she had cut into Daisy Duke shorts along with a grey tank top.

Who could be ringing my doorbell after dark? Maybe Ms. Barker wants me to open her medicine bottle again. Chloe wondered. Chloe peeped through the glass panes in the door but all she saw was a bouquet of flowers with what appeared to be a male standing behind the flowers. *Is that a man? Surely, not at my door.*

"Who is it?" She asked and held her breath.

"Me. Derrin." The husky voice sent chills up her spine even through the door.

Chloe, without hesitation, snatched the door open and was standing a mere foot from the man of her dreams.

"What are you doing here, Derrin? I thought we had our one and done." She was still slightly pissed at him.

"Hello to you, too." Derrin lowered the flowers and smiled at her showing his pearly white teeth that shone even brighter in the dusk of the night. His smiled melted the chill off Chloe's demeanor.

"I'm sorry. Please excuse my manners. Come in." Chloe pulled the door open a few more inches and moved two steps backwards. She fanned her left arm to show Derrin he could enter.

What are you doing? You are supposed to give her the flowers, apologize and leave. Derrin heard his inner thoughts but the smell of Chloe's body wash was overloading his brain cells. He slowly stepped inside. Chloe closed the door with her back to him. When she turned around Derrin had moved within inches of her body. She pulled at the strap of her tank top. Then she remembered she was sans bra. She decided to cross her arms over her chest before Derrin noticed her nipples were perking up to say hello to him. Too late. She could tell from the darkened gaze in his eyes that he noticed her breast changes.

"So are you happy to see me?" Derrin asked with the sexiest smile he could muster.

"Not really." Chloe said then shrugged her shoulders.

Derrin laughed and threw his head back. When he finished laughing he faced her, only this time he had ever so slightly moved closer to her.

"Are you sure about that? I think your two roommates are saying otherwise." He glanced at her breasts and raised his left eyebrow as a challenge. She knew wholeheartedly what he meant by her two roommates, but she wanted to play along.

"I don't have any roommates. I am home alone." She backed up and bumped into the front door.

Derrin inched closer and removed the space she attempted to place between them. He came so close that the paper wrapping of the bouquet touched the tip of her chin. Her breathing was labored as evidenced by the rise and fall of her chest. Her breasts looked so soft. He wondered if he blew on them whether they would harden into nubs. He eased his hand with the bouquet behind his back and inched closer. Chloe closed her eyes. She was holding her breath, but when Derrin moved his lips close to her face, she let out a deep breath. He was so close her breasts touched his shirt. Without opening her eyes, she moaned. Before she could ask her next question, his lips were planted on top of hers.

First, he softly kissed around the corners of her mouth, then he used his tongue to lick the edges of her top lip. She moaned again, only this time she unknowingly cracked her lips apart. Derrin acted swiftly and captured her tongue. He kissed her with all the passion he could muster. He tried to slow down his hunger, but he could not stop the force of his desire to consume her lips. Her tongue was soft and moist. She tilted her head and he pressed closer to her. The feeling of her tongue in his mouth was taking over his senses. Before he knew it he dropped the bouquet and grabbed both sides of her face. He was kissing her lips like they were supplying his first sip of water after returning from the desert. Her moans were driving him insane.

He moved his hands from her face to the small of her back then to her butt. He pulled her closer. He wanted her to feel his hard erection at the juncture of her thighs. He wanted her to know he wanted her when he was sober and wide awake.

Instantly his hands rubbed across her butt, his thumb latched onto the top edge of her shorts. He wiggled each of his fingers into the waist of her shorts. Within seconds, her right leg lifted from the floor and wrapped around his waist. She threw her head back and he lightly kissed her from her chin down to the base of her neck. This was not enough. He wanted to brand her as his. So, the light kisses became sucks and pulls.

Chloe mumbled, "Oh, Derrin."

As if his trigger had been pushed, he pulled her tank top up. His hands glided over her breasts. When he saw her twin mounds staring back at him in their lovely splendor, he quietly asked her, "Do you ever wear panties AND a bra?"

Before she could respond, he started kissing and sucking her tongue again. Any retort she was planning to give was smothered by his lips.

He had to taste her breasts first then he would taste the very essence of her. He placed his lips on her right breast first. He tugged at the nipple. He flicked his tongue over just the nipple then he put the entire areola in his mouth. Not getting enough, he began to suckle her nipples like a newborn. With each movement of his tongue, Chloe swung her head from side to side. The palms of her hands were pressed flat against the front door.

Derrin switched from the right breast to the left and passionately tortured her even more. Her breast glistened with the moisture from his tongue. Finally, Derrin pulled back and gazed in her eyes. *God she is beautiful.*

"Now that I have got a little taste of your roommates, I want to taste you." Chloe gasped as Derrin fell to his knees and pulled down her shorts and panties in one quick sweep. He moved so quickly he did not even see the color of her intimate coverings. He pressed his nose against the black soft curls covering her very essence. He inhaled deeply. Her aroused scent was driving him over the edge. But he came to apologize and this was the only way he knew how to communicate his thoughts. So, no release for him tonight, it was just for her.

Derrin placed his hand on the back of her right thigh and gently pulled her leg up around his neck. Then he eased her other leg away to the side slightly. She was wide open and ready for tasting. Derrin looked up at Chloe and she looked as though she was holding her breath. He wanted to make her scream. He set out to achieve his goal.

He used his thumbs to ease open her womanly folds. Then he glided his thumb across her center. She was wet, but not wet enough. He wanted her essence dripping down his tongue, across his lips, ending on his chin. Derrin was determined to quench his thirst for Chloe. Holding her hips firmly in his hand, Derrin lowered his mouth to her moist blossom and felt her body clench in surprise. Then she released the breath she was holding and made sounds of shocked pleasure erupting from deep in her throat.

His tongue delved into the very essence of her. First, he lapped, then licked and sucked her while his fingers entered her, thrusting in and out. He loved and enjoyed every second. He could feel the trembling of her thighs. As if he would ever consider leaving before he satisfied her, Chloe moved her hands from the door to his head.

Derrin used slightly quicker and more forceful movements to lap her into an orgasm. The shutters began and Chloe moaned, "Yes!"

She felt surges and surges of sensations moving through every part of her body. And then she felt it, the force of a hurricane washing over her as he continued to stroke her to oblivion. Her body splintered into a thousand pieces as an orgasm ripped through her, almost snatching her breath away. Then after he had taken her over the edge, she slumped over and slid down the door to the floor. Derrin stared at her and basked in the knowledge of knowing he gave her such great pleasure.

"So do you accept my apology?" Derrin said before forming a wide smile.

"If that was an apology, I will accept it every time. But what are you apologizing for?" Chloe said breathing so deep she thought she was having an asthma attack. She ran her hand over her face and hair. She was soaking wet from sweat.

"I wanted to let you know that I did not regret that first night with you. While, I did not find the best words to express my thoughts that night, I was just trying to let you know that I did not force myself on you. But my words got tangled up when I was looking at how beautiful you were with your after sex glow. My bad." Chloe blushed and her caramel colored face turned a soft red.

Derrin stood to his feet and pulled Chloe up by one arm. He then proceeded to lower her tank top back over her breasts and pulled her panties and shorts back up. He slowly dusted her off, taking his time when he touched her butt and thighs. Chloe was mesmerized by his thoughtfulness. She was also speechless.

"I hope I am not interrupting anything. What were you doing before I rang your doorbell?" He asked as he glanced around the room.

"I was about to eat some spaghetti I cooked and watch a movie. Do you want to eat something?" Derrin raised one brow and grinned.

Chloe blushed when she realized the sexual innuendo.

Derrin chuckled. "I *have* worked up an appetite. If you don't mind the company, I think I will have a plate."

"No problem. One plate of Chloe-getti coming up." Chloe smiled then walked past Derrin with a little more sway in her hips than necessary. From the view of her back, he had no idea she was grinning like a Cheshire cat.

Derrin crossed the foyer and entered the formal dining room. He closed the blinds to keep the glare of the street lights out of the house. He heard the beeping of the microwave in the distance.

Wow. I know I'm not going to get any sleep now. This was better than any dream. Take it easy or you will get caught up and fall for her. Derrin thought as he released a deep, heavy breath.

You need a game plan. And it needs to be better than one and done. That is not going to work for this beauty.

The noise from the forks tapping the plates brought his attention back to the room. Chloe was entering with two plates of spaghetti with meatballs and a salad.

"If you want, we can eat in the family room and watch TV. I rarely sit in here when I am home alone.

"Are you home alone often?" Derrin asked with a sincere inquisitive stare.

"Put it like this, other than my friends, Kenya and Cara, my cousin Diane, my mother who lives in South Atlanta, and you, I have not had any other company here in the three years I have owned the place."

"Am I the only male who has had the pleasure of your company in three years?" Derrin gently removed one plate from her hands and sat down. He never let his gaze leave her eyes. He wanted to see her reaction to his question.

"Derrin, let's not play games. You and I both know, in great detail, I might add, that you are the only male who has given me any pleasure in all my years not just the last three. But if you are asking if I date, then the answer is sometimes. I just never found anyone worthy to bring to my home." Derrin's eyes darkened and his sexual desire lit his entire face.

Chloe shuddered, remembering just what kind of pleasure he could deliver. Nervously biting the corner of her bottom lip, Chloe tried to eat her spaghetti. She was suffering from a temporary loss of words as she sat trying not to look at Derrin. He was the most gorgeous man she had ever laid eyes on. She could not believe that in two weeks she had experienced over the top sex with a man who never seemed to notice her before. She wanted to pinch herself to make sure she wasn't imagining the whole thing.

She knew Derrin claimed he came by just to apologize, but in her mind she kept asking why did he make love to her and why was he still here. She did not have the answers to any of her questions. What she did have were tremors in her legs from the last orgasm she had the pleasure of experiencing against the door in her foyer, of all places. Chloe's mind was whirling in a million directions. She wasn't sure if she was supposed to chat with Derrin like nothing happened or if she should try to seduce him. After pondering this issue, she decided she was ill prepared to seduce him due to her lack of experience. She determined she would act like he was a good friend. She rubbed her hand across her stomach to calm her nerves. She was going to do her best acting job ever. She was going to show him she was not interested in him one bit. Chloe eased her head up and looked directly into Derrin's eyes.

Not wanting the moment to become sexually charged again, she smiled and rose to her feet. She picked up her plate before speaking.

"Let's go in the den. I really want to watch one of my rented movies tonight. I have to take it back to the Blockbuster kiosk by tomorrow."

"Okay. What movies did you get, some chick flicks?" Derrin grabbed his plate and swung one leg over his seat as he followed Chloe to the den.

"It depends on whether you think a movie about the Rwandan genocide entitled 'Sometimes in April' or the horror movie 'The Reaping' to be chick flicks." She swayed her hips a little more as she sashayed into the den. Derrin tried unsuccessfully to keep his mind off making love to her again, but with each step made and every sway of her hips it was becoming harder to fight the urge. Her five foot eight frame was perfect for her small waist and round butt. She was the ideal body type for his tastes.

"I think I saw 'The Reaping'. It is not really scary and I definitely wouldn't call it a horror movie." Derrin paused as Chloe crossed her legs under her body and sat down on the black loveseat. From the way she had centered herself on the sofa, he figured she did not want to share her space. He was left with sitting on the matching sofa.

"Well, we can watch 'Sometimes in April' if you have already seen 'The Reaping'. I haven't seen either."

"Hey, wait a minute. Isn't Idris Elba in both those movies?" Derrin realized that even though Chloe tried to give the impression that these movies were not chick flicks, they both had the same leading man in them. A man who women drooled over.

Chloe shrugged her shoulders trying to pretend to be nonchalant. "That is a coincidence, isn't it?" She said as she kept her eyes on the television. She was fighting hard to keep her lips from forming a wide devious grin. She knew Idris Elba was a woman's dream. *Move over Denzel Washington, Idris is coming through*, she thought.

"Oh, so I'm going to have to sit here and watch you drool over another guy. Man, that's cruel." Derrin softly laughed.

Chloe pressed the buttons on the remote and the movie started. She sat back and ate her meal for the first few minutes. Then once she was finished she noticed that Derrin was also finished. She rose from the loveseat and gently tugged on his plate.

"Do you want something to drink? I have wine, beer, and red Kool-Aid." Without hesitation, Derrin requested Kool-Aid.

"You do know red is a color not a flavor." Derrin retorted. Chloe had quickly exited the den and was placing the dishes in the kitchen sink. She used this time to gather her thoughts and wits. She had only seen a few minutes of the movie and already she wanted to throw caution to the wind and kiss Derrin's sexy lips. She could not wait for him to finish eating. Each time his lips landed on the fork, Chloe felt shivers at the thoughts of what his lips could do. She rubbed her hands down the sides of her shorts. She retrieved two glasses from the dishwasher and poured the beverages. She thought she heard Derrin talking but she could not really make out what he was saying. She picked up the glasses and returned to the den. She had a cooler calmer demeanor.

Derrin wanted to tease Chloe about the common African American cultural reference to Kool-Aid by the color not the flavor. He began by saying in a voice loud enough for her to hear in the kitchen. "Chloe, I'm sure the marketing department at Kool-Aid is losing sleep over their flavor names and marketing techniques to prevent you from referring to cherry, strawberry, raspberry, tropical punch and the all time favorite watermelon as red Kool-Aid."

Chloe re-entered the den. She was not fazed by his comments.

"Whatever. You know what I meant. Red Kool-Aid is the flavor I was raised to call it so that's what it is. The marketing department just cares that we are buying the packets like crazy. They could care less that we call it red Kool-Aid." Then she stuck out her tongue like she was a ten year old kid.

"Alright don't get anything started you may not want to finish." Derrin had scooted to the edge of the sofa, hoping that she would give him a sign, even a small sign that she was game for round two. She just plopped down on the sofa and rewound the movie. This time she was sitting in the corner of the loveseat. Derrin seized the opportunity to move closer to Chloe. He slid down on the floor and stretched out. He noticed Chloe watching him out of the corner of her eye. He stretched and pretended to yarn. Then he asked, "Can I take my shoes off? My feet are starting to hurt."

Chloe looked at his feet and figured they probably were hurting since he had on heavy work boots.

"Sure. Make yourself at home."

Derrin removed his shoes but when he laid the second one down on the carpet, he decided to get up and sit on the opposite end of the loveseat instead of the sofa.

"What are you doing?" Chloe asked inquisitively.

"You said to make myself at home, so I moved to the loveseat. It looks more comfortable than the sofa over there." He then stretched his legs out, but not without placing one foot behind Chloe's back and placing the other one in her lap. He could tell she was slightly aroused by having his foot in her lap with his heel firmly settled on the center of her womanhood.

"No funny games, mister." Chloe recognized the beginnings of his seduction.

"Of course not. I was just getting comfortable." Then he laid back, placed his hands behind his neck and turned to face the television.

For the next two hours, Derrin watched the movie as the characters hurriedly tried to leave the city or find missing loved ones. He was captivated by the story. Before tonight, he had no idea the Rwandan people were in a civil war. Every so often he glanced at Chloe. At times she was wiping tears from her cheeks while at other times her eyes were filled with lust. He knew she was attracted to Idris Elba. However, whenever her eyes met his, the lust would vanish. Derrin had never experienced this type of reaction from a woman, especially not one he had slept with before. He was especially disappointed when she did not react to his efforts to wiggle his toes around her breasts and the juncture of her thighs. He might as well had been a lap puppy. She was unfazed by his efforts to slightly seduce her. He could have moved closer and kissed her, but he wanted her to initiate things since he came over just to apologize not make love to her again. For the second time in his life, he was undesired by a woman. Thoughts of Nicole Barker made him tense. The heel of his foot accidentally kicked Chloe.

"Ow. What was that for?" Chloe said as she rubbed her leg with both her hands.

Derrin snapped out of his trance and realized his ex-fiancé was still controlling him like a puppet. *Damn her.*

"I'm okay. I am just a little sleepy. I think I need to be leaving anyway. I have to get up early to open the café." Derrin sat up and moved his legs to the front of the loveseat. As he began putting his shoes back on, he took one last gaze at Chloe.

"Chloe, I have to admit I really enjoyed myself tonight. I hope you will invite me over again."

"Of course, I will. In fact, you have a standing invitation to come over and watch movies with me any time you like." There she said it. She made the comment as nonchalantly as possible. Derrin's smile slowly moved from the edges of his lips to spread across his face. *You have no idea of the gift you just gave me.* He thought.

He moved toward the foyer and turned to face Chloe.

"Like I said, I really enjoyed myself tonight. I hope you did too."

Chloe refrained from saying *I most certainly did.* Instead, she responded with, "It was fun."

She opened the door and he stepped out onto the porch. She softly closed the door behind him and watched from the side of the curtains until he was out of her line of view.

CHAPTER FIVE

Chloe nearly melted into a pool of water as she remembered everything that transpired between the time she opened the door to Derrin and when she closed it behind him. She never believed in a million years that she would have one night of wonderful sex with him let alone two nights. Chloe walked back to her sofa and dropped down on it. She wanted to tell someone maybe it would seem real and not imagined if she could share the evening with someone else.

Chloe knew just the person, Kenya. She picked up the receiver from the phone cradle, but as she began pressing the buttons for Kenya's phone number, she wondered if Kenya was the best person. *She is Derrin's sister.* Chloe placed the phone back on the cradle. She pondered the situation more closely.

Think. Okay. I cannot call Diane she is going through her "I hate men because they all lie and cheat" phase. She will probably think Derrin is secretly married or living with a baby's mama or something worst. Cara is not really keen on the idea that Derrin was the reason I left the party crying. She swears I am just covering for him when I say he did not do anything wrong. Of course, I did not tell her that I gave my virginity up to him. What she does not know won't hurt me. Chloe softly chuckled at the thought of Cara learning she waited so long to give her virginity up in the first place.

Kenya is my best friend. She already knows I am in love with her brother. She also knows something happened to cause me to leave the party that night. She knows better than anyone how it feels to finally be with the one you love. She knows Derrin too. He is a big boy and can handle any woman he comes into contact with.

After careful deliberation, Chloe dialed Kenya's number. With each ring of the phone line butterflies fluttered in her stomach. She did not have to endure the nervousness long. Kenya answered on the third ring.

"Hey, Chloe. What's up?" Kenya sounded like she was out of breath.

Chloe responded, "Nothing much. I just needed to talk to you about something. Do you have a minute?" Chloe began twirling the single curl that fell to the side of her face.

"Girl, yes I have time. You caught me just at the right moment. I was going to call you earlier but I needed to finish a workout before I called. You know we can stay on the phone for hours. What's going on?" Kenya had an idea but wanted to see how Chloe was going to raise the subject.

"Well, you know how I have been hard on the guys who try to take me out on dates, right?"

Not expecting this to be the lead in for the conversation, Kenya hesitated before responding. "Yeah."

"Uh, I am thinking that I should go easy on them now. I will never get a steady date if I keep turning them away or finding a reason to block their number from my phone, especially since I am not a virgin anymore. I figured there is nothing to cherish or be scared of, you know what I mean?"

"Whoa. You were rambling like tumbleweed in the desert. Are you saying you lost your virginity? Where have I been? I know I did not miss that event." Kenya teased Chloe in an effort to calm Chloe down. She could tell Chloe was nervous by the rapid pace at which she blurted the statements out.

"You did not miss anything. I lost my virginity about two weeks ago. I was just keeping it to myself." Chloe stopped twirling the curl and closed her eyes. She inhaled very deeply and thought to herself *It's now or never.*

"Kenya I slept with Derrin at the party. He was sleep and I was knocked out on headache medicine and it just happened. I'm sorry;

31

please don't be mad at me. You are my best friend and if I can't share the details of the happiest night of my life, well the second happiest night of my life, then I am just going to die. Please say its okay, please." Chloe finally released the breath she was holding.

"Oh, so that's why you kept this a secret. You gave up the goodies to Derrin. Good for you." Kenya covered her mouth to keep from laughing into the phone. She knew she had to play along and pretend she had no idea or Chloe would be suspicious.

"Wait a minute, Chloe. If that was the second most happiest night of your life what topped it on your list?" Kenya was lying across her bed. Now she sat up. Something was telling her Derrin was involved in the answer.

Chloe bit her lip and closed her eyes. "Tonight was the best night ever." No one said anything for about two seconds. Kenya finally broke the silence.

"What happened tonight? You know I am on pins and needles over here."

Chloe opened one eye and said in rapid pace, "Derrin came over to apologize for his comments that upset me that night. Well before I could take the flowers from him, he kissed me senseless. Then one thing led to another and he said he wanted to taste me. So he did. All over. All ... over, if you know what I mean."

"Ew, nasty. I do not want to hear about the sexual adventures you have with my brother." Kenya laughed and paused. Then she continued. "But if you are happy so am I." Kenya made a mental note to kill her brother as soon as she ended this call with Chloe. He was not supposed to be intimate with her again. But Kenya just had to get an answer to the million dollar question.

"Chlo, what do you think this means for you and Derrin?"

"Absolutely nothing. I know he is a one and done type of guy. He only stars in dreams and easy flings. I have no expectations of forever after with Derrin."

"Okay. Just so you know how he operates. But ... I will say if there is any woman who can get him to change his way of thinking it may very well be you, Chloe Dancy. You just might be the one for him."

"Child please. Derrin is looking for a relationship like he is looking for a hole in his head. I am satisfied with my two nights with him. There is no need to test reality."

"I hear you Chlo. I'm just saying. Derrin needs a real woman and not some booty call or gold digger. He used to want a wife and family. He could want it again if you work hard on him."

Chloe was silent. She was at a loss for words. Her best friend actually was attempting to encourage a relationship with her brother. Surely this was just a part of the continuous dream she was having.

"Thanks, Ken for the vote of confidence but Derrin is not looking for me. He gave me more than I could have imagined. He even said he liked my spaghetti.

"What spaghetti?" Kenya was frowning up now.

"I made spaghetti and he ate dinner with me then he stayed and watched one of my Idris Elba movies."

"Are you saying my brother, the infamous commitment-phobe, actually hung around with you like you and he were a couple on a date?" Kenya once again covered her mouth. This time she was trying to keep her squeals of joy from coming out of her throat.

"No, it was not like a date. I had cooked and was going to watch the movie anyway. He had a plate just not to be rude. I am sure that was the reason. A date was the farthest thing from his mind." Chloe was horrified. She did not want Kenya to describe the evening as a date. Derrin would be sure to get pissed. Chloe needed to act fast.

"Kenya, promise me that you won't tell Derrin that I told you about tonight. Please."

"Alright. I won't." Kenya assured her then easily changed the subject to get Chloe back in her comfort zone. "Chlo, let's talk about these new guys you are going to give a chance to win your heart."

They continued to talk about their plans to go out on the town next weekend.

Before they ended the call, Kenya wanted to confirm their plans. "So, next weekend it will be girl's night? You think we should invite Diane and Cara?"

"I guess we can invite them, but I doubt Diane would go to a game night. She would question our sanity for attending an event for singles where all you do is play games, like Twister, Spades, Monopoly, Candyland, and Charades. And Cara, humph. She would want to add stripping to the rules of each game. We can ask but I don't know how it will turn out."

"Ken I don't care how they act. If I can leave the event with a future date, I will be more than happy. We will have to toast to new beginnings."

"Sounds like a plan. Talk to you later." They both hung up the phones.

Kenya immediately waited for a dial tone and called Derrin. The phone just rang and then his voicemail picked up.

"Call me. I want to know if Chloe accepted your apology. I am sure you are rolled up with your next conquest, but call me tomorrow. Holla."

CHAPTER SIX

D errin was lying on his leather couch when Kenya called. He knew she wanted details on how things went. He just was not prepared to tell her that he smelled Chloe's body wash and lost all his senses. He was a little embarrassed and he knew his sister would chew him up and spit him out if he told her what happened by the front door. He decided to let her leave a message. He will deal with her tomorrow.

He intentionally tuned his television to the Discovery channel. He wanted to fall asleep to the sounds of birds chirping. He settled for an animal show about bee harvesting. He had no interest in bees. *The birds and the bees, maybe.* He grinned and then closed his eyes.

Nearly four hours later, he awoke to the sounds of a military raid complete with air strikes and missiles. The television was blasting the sounds in a war documentary. He rose from the sofa and went to his bed. It was close to four o'clock in the morning. It would be time for him to leave for his morning run soon. He wanted to get just a few more minutes of sleep. He closed his eyes and there she was. Chloe was back in his dreams more vividly than ever. But instead of hoping to get rid of her, he wanted to bask in her company. Her laughter made his heart beat faster. He wanted to savor this dream. Or was it a fantasy? He did not know and right now he did not care.

He finally rose and began his day. For the next three days, Derrin dreamed and fantasized about Chloe. He was anxious to get home each day kick off his shoes and lay down to think about Chloe.

He was surprised that the days had passed without him so much as wanting to call another woman. But his body was beginning to tell him he needed to expend some sexual energy. His heart had no desire to satisfy another woman. His mind told him to get up and go out with his boys. However, this was hard to do when his body wanted him to go back to Chloe's house and lay his head in her lap.

Lay my head in her lap. I must be cracking up. Did I eat today? I could be suffering from low blood sugar. They say low blood sugar can cause delusions. Yeah, low blood sugar, that's it.

Derrin sat up on the couch and pulled out his cell phone to call his friend Jared. He noticed he had five missed calls from Kenya. He still had not called her back. He was waiting for her to show up and punch him in his stomach. He dialed Jared, but the phone went straight to voicemail. Derrin decided to drive toward Jared's house and see if Jared wanted to go to the Taco Mac for drinks. There were always pretty wanton girls at the Taco Mac.

As Derrin headed to the ramp for the expressway, he suddenly turned onto State Road 400 North in the direction of Chloe's house. Before he could think through his decision, he was pulling into her driveway. He should have called but come to think of it he did not have her phone number. He needed to correct that minor oversight.

He turned off his car and exited. He glanced around to see if he was being watched by the neighbors. While, he did not see anyone, he had a feeling that someone's grandmother was writing down his license plate and description just in case. The thought made him chuckle.

He pressed the doorbell but suddenly moved from the view of the window. He had to come up with a reason for being at Chloe's doorstep before she came to the door.

Think. I was just passing through. No. I was in the neighborhood. Not. I left my earring. Hell that was the excuse the women he slept with gave for showing up at his loft uninvited. Plus, he did not wear his diamond earring anymore. It was a fad that had long played out in his book.

"Who is it? Ms. Barker is that you?" Before she waited for a response, Chloe swung the wood door open and stepped out onto the porch. "Ms. Barker?" She turned to her left and met Derrin's gaze.

Startled she jumped and pressed her right hand over her heart.

"Oh, you scared me. What are you doing out here? Why didn't you say anything?" Chloe crossed her arms over her chest and patted her foot waiting for an answer.

"I like the element of surprise. I didn't intend to scare you though. I simply wanted to surprise you. Surprise." Derrin put his hands in his pockets, his telltale habit when he was nervous.

"Surprise? Who said I liked surprises?"

"Doesn't everyone like surprises?" He slowly began to glide over to stand in front of Chloe. He continued talking in his deepest baritone voice. "I wanted to see you so I thought I would stop by to surprise you. Don't be mad. Plus, I was really thirsty for some red Kool-Aid. You know they don't sell that flavor in Alpharetta where I live."

She cracked a smile. Derrin then added, "Plus, I didn't have your phone number to call you."

Chloe could not hold her amusement much longer. She moved toward the door and walked back into her house. She made sure not to pause at the door like she had done on his last visit. Derrin quietly followed Chloe, thankful that she did not turn him away. He knew if the tables were turned he would have sent an uninvited woman who appeared on his doorstep right back to where she came from.

Chloe reached her den and turned around to face Derrin. "I have to make some red Kool-Aid. You can wait in here. The remote is over on the sofa, if you want to change the channel." Derrin glanced at the remote and the television. He had no intention of sitting down watching television without Chloe. He looked back at Chloe and responded.

"I think I will go and help you make the Kool-Aid, if you don't mind." Derrin smiled and flashed his teeth. Chloe paused a few seconds before shrugging her shoulders in indifference.

"Okay. But I don't think I need much help stirring sugar and water." She eased into the kitchen and walked to the large food pantry. When she was in the pantry, Derrin took the opportunity to assess the surroundings. The kitchen was extremely large for one person. There were oak wood cabinets throughout with coordinated blinds in the bay window. The dining table, which was large enough for six people, was decorated with casual place settings and a large artificial floral arrangement in the center. If there was a theme to the decorations, Derrin would guess it would be purple grapes since there were grapes on the back splash, and various grape figures scattered throughout.

Derrin felt comfortable and at home. This scared him. His palms began to feel damp.

Chloe returned to the kitchen with three small round containers of Kool-Aid. She attempted to appear cheerful, but internally she was worried. She did not want to fall prey to Derrin's please them and leave them routine, but she could not help wanting to be around him at all times. She was fighting the urge to fall deeper in love with him.

She placed the containers on the table one at a time.

"I have watermelon, cherry and strawberry flavors. So which red Kool-Aid do you want?" Chloe smiled. She made eye contact with Derrin and her stomach fluttered.

Derrin rubbed his chin and leaned back against the counter.

"Hmm. Let me see." He paused and then grinned at her. "Cherry. I like popping cherries." Derrin smirked and coughed to keep from laughing when he saw Chloe's reaction. He could tell she was surprised by his remark as evidenced by the way her face was turning red.

Chloe swallowed hard before she began speaking.

"Derrin why are you here? Surely, it's not for Kool-Aid, especially since the packs cost about twenty-five cents."

Derrin looked directly into her eyes. "To be honest, I don't know. All I do know is that I wanted to see you and hear your voice. So, here I am."

Chloe studied him for a few moments then she replied. "Interesting. I thought this was a booty call."

"Do you want it to be? You know I aim to please." Derrin said as he moved closer to Chloe to shorten the distance between them. Chloe sucked on her bottom lip and looked away toward the sink. She contemplated Derrin's question and decided it would not hurt to just talk. By the time she rotated her head back to face Derrin, he was standing directly in front of her. Her gaze met his and she licked her lips. "No, I don't want to be a booty call, Derrin but I would love to just talk."

Derrin mustered all the control he had to keep from kissing Chloe, but the more she nervously licked and sucked her lips he was losing his control. Before he reneged on his statement that this was not a booty call, he decided he would get to know her. He reached down and grabbed her hand. He gently guided her to the den.

"The Kool-Aid can wait. Let's talk. I want to get to know you. I need to figure out my fascination with Chloe Dancy." Derrin ignored the tingling sensation he felt when their hands touched. Her hands were soft and appeared small compared to his he observed as he guided her to the loveseat.

"Tell me three silly facts about you, Chloe that few people know. It can be your likes, dislikes or pet peeves just anything about you." Derrin sat next to her on the sofa with his right leg partially bent as he faced her. Chloe twisted her head slightly toward the ceiling and began thinking. After a few moments, she smiled and looked at Derrin.

"Okay, I will tell you, but you have to promise not to laugh." Derrin could tell from her expression that whatever she had in mind was going to be comical.

"Nope. I can't promise not to laugh. I will promise not to tell anyone. But if it is funny, I will laugh."

"Well, if you promise not to tell anyone. I guess I can live with that." Chloe crossed her legs on the sofa and began.

"I have this thing about my bare feet touching certain surfaces.

When I go outside barefooted, I can't just walk across the grass, I have to walk on my heels. The same thing happens when I walk on cold wood floors. If my toes touch the cold wood, I cringe."

Derrin was grinning. "Let me get this straight. You don't like your toes to touch the floor or grass? What other surface?" He was fighting the laugh that was bubbling in his throat.

"Hmm." Chloe thought hard about the answer to the question. "I can walk on wet sand just not dry sand. I can't take it." At that moment, Derrin let out a loud chuckle.

"You've got to be kidding me, right?" When Chloe shook her head, he continued. "Okay, give me another fact about you."

Chloe snapped her fingers and said, "I got one. When I eat bread I don't eat the edges. Instead of cutting off the edges, I just eat from the middle of the slice. I do that with cake too."

Derrin was laughing and shaking his head.

"Let me get this right, you leave a hole in the bread after you finish. Wow. Okay, one more fact. Make it a good one."

Chloe was giggling at the silly information she was sharing. "Okay. Final fact. I don't like to hold babies under a year old. I am afraid I will drop them and can't replace them. I have to carry them on a pillow. This really has not been a problem, but I wonder what will happen when I have children of my own." Chloe laughed and continued, "I will probably need therapy just to bring the baby home from the hospital." When she finished she looked at Derrin. He was starring at her bewildered.

Derrin did not know how to ask his next question, but the mention of a baby made him recall his dream and their failure to use protection.

"Uh, Chloe. Now that you mentioned holding babies, is it possible that you will only have nine months to get over your fear of holding babies?" Derrin watched her expression change from lightheartedness to concern.

"At the rate I'm going I will have nine years before I have to worry about my phobia. Why do you think I only have nine months?" She sincerely inquired. "You realize we did not use any protection that first night. Unless you are on birth control, you, no we, will have to get you some therapy soon." Derrin forced a grin while he twisted his hands waiting for Chloe respond.

Chloe immediately laughed. "Is that the real reason you came over to see me? Are you trying to see if I am pregnant? Well, let me inform you that I am not pregnant. Not that it is any of your concern, but I have had a cycle since our first encounter. So rest your nerves. You are not going to be a father and I will not need therapy to hold a baby any time soon." Chloe watched Derrin as he processed what she had just shared.

After a few moments of silence, Chloe decided to change the subject. "Now, it's your turn. Tell me three silly facts about you that very few people know." She adjusted her legs while Derrin rubbed his thighs. She patiently waited for him to spill the beans.

"Oh, this is easy. First, I am allergic to tomatoes. My body begins to feel like bugs are crawling under my skin if I even get a drop of the juice in my mouth. It's actually weird." Derrin was concentrating on his allergy memories. Chloe gasped.

"But I fed you spaghetti. Were you sick?" She covered her mouth with her hand and wondered what he was going to say. *Surely he wouldn't have eaten something that could potentially kill him.*

"No-o-o. I can eat cooked tomatoes not raw tomatoes. So you can calm down. I did not let you poison me. But that would have been good blackmail material."

"Whew. It's good to know you are allergic to raw tomatoes."

Derrin relaxed and removed his shoes. He was getting comfortable. He even pulled his shirt from inside his pants. Chloe watched with baited breath. His movement was quick but not fast enough to prevent a glimpse of the curly black hair at the base of his stomach area leading lower inside his pants. Chloe diverted her attention from his stomach back to their conversation. She fanned her hands like she was encouraging him to continue.

"Silly fact number two, would be... let me think. Oh, I know how to cross stitch. I have a picture I made hanging in my living room on the wall over my sofa."

"Cross-stitch? You mean where you make pictures and designs by stitching threads into a piece of fabric?"

"Exactly." Derrin said matter of fact.

"I need to ask this question. Why do you know how to cross-stitch? I am certain that was not the in thing for young males growing up in Atlanta." Chloe was smirking as she responded to Derrin.

Derrin looked off into the open space of the dining room across the hall. He seemed deep in thought. He was remembering something that brought back raw memories. When he turned back to face Chloe he answered her question.

"My Dad had a heart attack when I was a sophomore in high school. My Mom did not want to talk about the emotions she was feeling. She just wanted to sit and rock in a chair in his hospital room. I wanted to step up and be the man of the house. I wanted to protect her and Kenya, who was only in the sixth grade at the time.

Finally, I asked the hospital social worker what I could do to get my Mom to talk to me. She suggested a hobby. Being a student at the time, I researched hobbies and learned that cross-stitching, needlework, painting, photography, and pottery were good activities to encourage relaxation and easy conversation.

I purchased a few books and the supplies for a cross-stitch. Then I convinced my Mom that we needed to make a picture for Dad to put up in his hospital room. I told her it would help with his healing. She agreed.

In the beginning, she cross-stitched and I prepped the colored threads and helped her count the squares. Then she claimed she could not talk and cross-stitch at the same time. I think she was just wanted to see if I would do it. I did. It made her open up and ultimately helped her to discuss the pain and helplessness she felt with my Dad being sick." Derrin just stared at Chloe, who was speechless.

"Derrin, I am so sorry. I did not know your Dad had a heart attack. Kenya has never mentioned it and he looks great." She paused then added, "Now, you know you will have to cross-stitch something to prove you can do it. But you have to wait until I have my camera to capture it for my Facebook page." Chloe giggled at the thought of Derrin cross-stitching.

"Yeah, right. There is no way I am going to let you take a picture of me doing anything as girlie as cross-stitching. Mark that off your things to do list." Derrin swiped his hands across his neck to signal "cut" like the movie directors do when filming. Chloe was truly enjoying his company. She smiled at the thought that she was interacting more with Derrin in the last two weeks than she has in the entire eight years she has known him. She wanted to continue down this path, but it would be futile. Derrin was not the fall in love type.

"Okay, give me a final fact about Derrin Reynolds that few people know." Chloe edged him on.

"That's easy. You are looking at the Rosswood Elementary School spelling bee champ for the 1986-1987 school year." Derrin rose to his feet and did his best Rocky impression. At one point, he had his arms over his head pointing down toward his head.

"No applause. Don't push, all my fans will get a chance to touch the champ," he joked. Chloe was stretched out on the sofa cracking up laughing. She poked fun at his championship by batting her eyes and putting her hands in a praying position under her chin. She asked him for his autograph. "Please, may I have your autograph, Mr. Fifth Grade Spelling Bee Champ?"

Derrin stopped moving around. He tilted his head and pondered

Chloe's request. "Oh, you don't think I can spell. Well, you want to challenge me? Get the dictionary and bring it on. I know a lot of words." Chloe stopped laughing long enough to realize he was serious, then she burst out in laughter again.

"I don't think I have a dictionary. But if I find one you have a deal. We will have to bet on your ability to spell any word I pick from the dictionary." Chloe rose from the sofa and searched her bookshelf for a dictionary. She found her old college dictionary and returned to sit on the sofa.

"Okay, Webster. I have a dictionary. Let's get this challenge going." Derrin was bouncing on his toes and stretching his neck like he was warming up for a boxing match.

He stopped moving and asked Chloe a question. "What's in this for me? If I spell ten words correctly, what will I win?"

Chloe placed her index finger on her chin, acting as if she was seriously deliberating her response. She already knew what she wanted to give him, but she vowed to herself not to give in to sexual desires. She wanted to savor the wonderful memories she already had with Derrin. She remembered something he wanted from her but did not have. *I can give him my phone number.*

"For every word you spell correctly you get one digit of my phone number. If you want both my home and cell phone numbers you will have to spell twenty words correctly. Deal?" Chloe held out her pinky finger to seal the deal as if they were back in elementary school.

"Deal! This is going to be so easy." Derrin rubbed his hands together and sat on the sofa next to Chloe. The first word was easy, ménage à trois. Chloe moved to her second word, aphrodisiac. She had every intention to select as many sensual words as possible. Derrin spelled the both words correctly. He had a feeling he saw a theme developing.

"Uh, before we move forward, I need the first two digits of your phone number."

Chloe grinned. She was enjoying every minute of this.

"Seven Seven. Since you can guess the next number in the area code, I will give you a really easy word. Spell seduction."

"Funny. You know I can spell s-e-d-u-c-t-i-o-n. Next."

Chloe was going to make him work for the next digit.

"Well, spell titillating since you are so good." Derrin licked his lips and spelled the word correctly and with lightning speed. Chloe moved on to arousability followed by coitus and cunnilingus. After spelling these three words correctly, Derrin had won three more digits to Chloe's home phone number. He was getting sleepy and decided to lay his head in Chloe's lap as she held the dictionary she used to confirm his spelling was correct. When his head touched her thigh, Chloe slightly jumped, as this action startled her. The closer his face was to the center of womanhood, she tingled all over in anticipation.

However, Chloe continued announcing words for Derrin to spell without hesitation, but she was unsuccessful in her efforts to get him to miss a spelling. Within ten minutes he had obtained all the digits to her home phone number.

Since she did not want him to move his head from her lap she decided to challenge him to win the digits to her cell phone number. This time she would select medical terms or diseases. Derrin claimed he needed to carefully consider each of these words because he did not want to make a mistake. Before long, Chloe was rubbing her hand across Derrin's head and reading the definitions of some of the words she was selecting. With each stroke her nipples hardened. However, Chloe knew the words were long and boring. He closed his eyes to "envision the words, at least that's what he said. Soon he was fast asleep. Chloe enjoyed rubbing his head so she continued, shortly thereafter they were both asleep.

Chloe moved in her sleep and the edge of the dictionary pressed against her chin, which jarred her awake. She glanced down and noticed the dictionary was lying on her chest and Derrin's head was in her lap. She smiled. She enjoyed Derrin's company and conversation, but needed to wake him so she could go to the restroom. The clock on the fireplace read fifteen minutes past midnight. They must have fallen asleep during the spelling challenge. She grinned at the memory. She had a good time with Derrin in and out of the bed. But his kisses were to die for. Her lips and tongue melded to his lips whenever he kissed her. She longed for another kiss but she promised herself that they would just talk tonight. She could always use other ways to touch him. She rubbed her hand across his head. His hair was cut low but soft. She was mesmerized by his gorgeous facial structure even while he slept he was the most handsome man she knew. Chloe used her middle finger to trace the edges of his lips. He turned his face toward her stomach. Chloe's insides fluttered at the thought that he would wake up while she fantasized about his kisses. He was still asleep. She continued to trace his lips then she moved to his ears and eyebrows. She returned her index finger to touch his lips, then he quickly snapped her finger into his mouth. He gently sucked her finger. Chloe gasped. He sat up on his elbows and whispered in her ear. "You know if you want to touch me you don't have to wait until I'm asleep." He leaned back and gazed into her eyes.

Chloe could tell from the darkened look in his eyes that he wanted her. She peered out from her partially closed eyes to stare at his lips. She decided to throw caution to the wind and kiss him. Derrin knew without a shadow of a doubt that Chloe was going to kiss him. He wanted to wait patiently for her to initiate, but the heated anticipatory sensations he felt nearly made him leap up from the sofa. Before he could act on his urges, she lowered her mouth to his and eased her tongue between his lips. She wanted to seduce him.

The instant her lips touched his, he let out a groan. He quickly moved his arm behind her neck and rolled her under him. He lay on top of her. His erection was pressed at the juncture between her legs. His tongue was hot and slick which caused a sensory overload throughout her body. Derrin began sucking on her tongue, probing deeply yet gently throughout her mouth. She matched his effort and with each swipe of his tongue on her lips, she ached for him.

Derrin shifted the intensity of the kiss without warning. Her hips instinctively moved against his body and heat spread from her toes up through her belly. She wanted him and he wanted her. But right now, she needed air. She pulled back and took a deep breath. He licked his lips as if savoring the taste, then he slowly moved to a sitting position.

"Chloe, I told you this was not a booty call. I want you so bad my bones hurt. But I don't want to take advantage of your kindness." Chloe let out a long extended breath as he softly spoke.

"I promise we will continue this, just not tonight. Now walk me to the door before I lose my control and carry you into the bedroom." Chloe glided her hand over her neck in an effort to calm her nerves. She was pleasantly surprised by Derrin's statement. On the one hand she appreciated that he wanted to honor his promise not to turn his unexpected visit into a sexual quest, but right now her body craved him so much she could barely control the urge to attack him.

She rose and swiped at her shorts. He took her hand in his and walked toward the door. With each step, Chloe wondered if she would resort to begging in order to get him to stay. Her pride, which had been kicked to curb by her lust, finally suppressed the sexual desires that was running rampant throughout her body.

When they reached the door, Derrin turned around to face Chloe.

"Thank you for a great evening. I am glad you let me in. Now that I have your phone numbers, I will call you later. Perhaps we can go somewhere this weekend."

Chloe bit down on the corner of her bottom lip. She had plans for the weekend with Kenya and her girlfriends. She was participating in a girls' night out on the town which she hoped would lead to a steady relationship. She glanced up at Derrin and again met the darkened gaze of his eyes. The look in his eyes revealed that he was on the edge of releasing passion on her willing body.

"Well, maybe not this weekend. I'm going out to a singles event with Kenya."

"Oh." Derrin dryly replied. Derrin attempted to inquire without showing his disappointment that she was going out to meet men. "What singles' event are you all going to?" He smirked as if he knew they were looking for trouble or fun depending on how you viewed their plans.

"You know your sister is always exploring the new hip places. She has found this renovated art museum that hosts a Game event once a month. So we are going on Friday night." Chloe was excited even thinking about the event.

"A Game event, what's that?" Derrin squinted his eyes and frowned. He could only imagine what Kenya was getting them into.

"It's a place where you play mostly childhood games like Monopoly, Charades, Battlestar Galactica. The games are to help break the ice while you talk and get to know other singles. It sounds really fun."

"Yeah, right. Well I hope you have fun." Derrin exited the house and stepped out onto her porch. He stood there looking at her for a minute. Then finally he said, "Goodbye, Chloe."

She quickly responded, "Bye Webster." They both laughed at the implication that he was the dictionary enthusiast. He was still lightly chuckling when he got in his car and pulled away.

CHAPTER SEVEN

Derrin could not believe the place was packed. He thought the whole idea of a game night for singles was the silliest thing anyone could come up with. He definitely did not expect there to be this many people. The building was a converted three level brownstone. A drink bar was on the main and top levels. The dance floor was on the middle level. The owners had strategically placed gaming areas throughout the rooms. There were rooms for serious games, like Spades and there were rooms for the more animated games like charades. But there were also quite a few games from his early childhood days, including, Battlestar Galactica, Connect Four, and Twister. He overheard someone say there was even a room for spin the bottle.

He nursed a drink at the bar on the main level. He was hoping to give the impression that his appearance was just a coincidence instead of a planned tactical move. He knew Kenya, Chloe and their other two friends were coming. He arrived early in order to already be in place when they arrived. He was interested to see the type of men Chloe was attracted to. He also wanted to see firsthand if she enjoyed her evening.

He did not want to do anything to upset her, but he did not want to sit at home and wonder what she was doing either. Chloe sounded so excited about her plans to attend this event, so he encouraged her. He should have stuck to his guns and told her this was not a place for his woman to be. *His woman? Don't start.* Derrin pushed the thoughts that he wanted to claim any woman as his to the back of his mind. He was not falling for that trap again. Nicole had done a number on him and he vowed not to be played by a woman ever again. Derrin knew deep down within his soul that Chloe did not have any of the same gold digging and spirit killing ways like Nicole, but he was not planning to find out.

After nearly forty-five minutes of pretending to be interested in the women who approached him at the bar, Kenya and Chloe walked in. Derrin sipped his drink and watched Chloe over the rim of his glass. She was beautiful. He pretended to be interested in the vacation plans of the lady standing next to him. This particular woman had been talking to him for ten minutes, which was about nine minutes longer than he should have listened.

He could not take his eyes off Chloe. She was gorgeous in the burgundy knit one shoulder top. The top accentuated her breasts and casually lay over the top of her black hip hugging capri pants. But it was the rhinestone jeweled burgundy and gold strappy sandals that made his erection grow. He decided to let them get settled in. He eased up the stairs to visit the top level. He would make his rounds to all the rooms and effortlessly appear when Chloe least expected it.

It did not take long for Kenya, Chloe, Cara and Diane to get drinks and find a table on the middle level. They appeared as excited as children on Christmas Day.

Chloe was ready for action. She wanted to get someone to go with her to the game areas. Chloe asked, "Kenya what do you say, Charades or Twister? I am ready to have some fun." Chloe raised her right arm in the air and waved it around slightly. Before Kenya could respond, Cara said, "Well, I am going to play Spades. I feel like talking junk tonight. If a man can hold his own in Spades then he may have an easy lay tonight." Cara threw her head back and laughed. Diane just sat at the table and rolled her eyes.

"Cara, let's stay together first. Once we get accumulated then we can separate. Since we are on this level let's try one of the games here." Chloe interjected.

"I vote for Twister. It can be very touchy feely." Kenya proclaimed with a wicked grin.

"Okay. Let's go. It looks like a new game is about to start." Cara proudly stated with a grin that stretched her lips across her entire face.

Diane, the scrooge of the group, informed them all, "I will sit here and watch the drinks. You all go on. I'm going to sit this one out."

The women pranced off to mix and mingle with the other players. Besides the three of them, there were at least four men and one additional lady. They had more than enough to play a long round of Twister. While everyone stood around the edges of the two Twister mats, the hostess explained the rules to refresh everyone's recollection of how the game was played. She reminded them that she would call a body part and color and they had to place the body part on the designated color without allowing their knees, elbows or bodies to touch the mat. Then the hostess split the players into four teams of two. Each team had a male and female. The hostess started two games simultaneously. Initially, the four teams squared off in separate games. Chloe was happy to be partnered with a six foot two creamy brown Adonis. He wore his hair in short twists. His tan shirt clung to his muscles. He looked like he was heavily into weight training. Chloe smiled at him and introduced herself. "Hello, I am Chloe. You are?" The high pitched voice that came from his mouth was definitely a turnoff. "Hi Chloe, I'm Russell, but you can call me Russ just so long as you call me." Chloe smirked. She could not believe his line was so lame. The hostess slightly twisted the bell in her hand to let the players know the game was beginning.

The referees stood by each mat and monitored the game.

"Right hand – Red" was the first move to initiate the game. The game progressed quickly. Cara was eliminated after the third move because she was too busy trying to land under the guy on the opposing team. Cara went back to the table and winked at Kenya. Kenya tried to keep from laughing and was eliminated when her elbow touched the mat. She too rose from the mat and went back to the table. Slowly all, but three players were eliminated from the game, Chloe, Russ and a lady named Sharon. Chloe was in a position with her legs spread apart so that her toes were on the colored circles and her left hand was flat on the yellow circle to her left. She had her right hand behind her back. She looked as if she was going to do a one armed push up. Russ was partially under her with his left arm stretched to a circle almost directly under her stomach. He was on his back with his left leg up in the air. Derrin appeared on the third floor landing and watched the game as it continued.

"Left leg – Green" was the next move. Chloe moved with lightning speed to put her left leg on the green circle beside her. Her foot made it before Sharon's. Sharon's knee touched the mat and she was eliminated. As Sharon was rising from the floor, Derrin came down the stairs. He was watching the game for a few minutes but then something clicked and he realized that Chloe was smiling while she was hovering over a guy. Derrin could not believe that she was playing a game where she would be placed in compromising positions in public. Anger flooded his mind and he quickly moved down the stairs, slightly pushing people out of his way. Before he could spell Mary Poppin's "superfragilisticexpialidocious," he was standing at the edge of the game mat staring at Chloe. Chloe was oblivious to his presence, as she was concentrating on winning the game. His sudden appearance did not get past Kenya, even though she was seated at the table farthest from the game.

Kenya watched Derrin. Something about his demeanor did not seem normal. If she was a betting woman, she would bet he was jealous of Chloe and the guy on the Twister mat. *Surely I am imagining things.* Kenya thought to herself. Cara's voice ended Kenya's deliberation.

"Ken, isn't that your brother. What is he doing over by Chloe?

Diane sipped her drink and casually commented. "It seems he does not like seeing Chloe all twisted up with the fine brother pressing his mouth near her lips. I could be wrong, ... but I doubt it." Diane was slurring her words by the time she finished the sentence. She clearly had one too many drinks.

The hostess called out the next move, "Right hand – Blue." Chloe moved her right arm from behind her back and Russ scooted backwards and placed his right hand on the nearest blue circle under Chloe. Russ pursed his lips as if he was going to whistle. He blew air on Chloe's bare shoulder. The action startled Chloe and she fell, right on top of Russ. They both laughed. Then Russ said to Chloe, "I could learn to love this position." Chloe smiled. But she could not respond before Derrin had grabbed her by the arm and pulled her off the guy. She was taken by surprise when she realized she was no longer lying on Russ. She glanced up and stared directly into Derrin's eyes. She saw desire shining through his dark brown eyes. But she also saw anger. She had no idea what happened, but something had pissed Derrin off.

"Chloe, put your shoes on we're leaving." Chloe did not move she was paralyzed by his possessive actions. When she did not move, Derrin softly grabbed her hand and pulled her to the table where her friends were seated.

"Kenya, give Chloe her purse. She's leaving. She will call you tomorrow." Kenya jumped to her feet and put one hand on her hip. "Derrin, who died and made you the boss? Plus, how do you know Chloe didn't drive us here?" Derrin looked over his shoulder at a stunned Chloe and asked, "Did you drive here tonight?"

Chloe found her voice and responded. "No." She was still speechless though. She took her sandals from Diane and mouthed, "thank you."

Derrin turned back to his sister and said. "We are leaving before I punch that dude for being presumptuous with Chloe." Derrin moved to the side and stepped backwards to put distance between him and Kenya.

Kenya's mouth fell open and she started to respond when she realized her brother was falling for Chloe. No, he probably won't admit it or acknowledge the fact, but he was definitely smitten. Kenya closed her mouth and smirked. Derrin did not notice because he was too busy watching Chloe hold on to the table with one hand and slip her sandals on with the other hand.

Chloe did not know how to react. She was confused, on the one hand she wanted to be pissed at how he was acting but on the other she was flattered that Derrin was seemingly jealous of this random guy. She took her time putting her sandals back on so she could contemplate her next action. Chloe finally had both sandals on. She felt empowered by the stilettos.

She calmly reached down on the table and picked up her drink. She commented directly into the glass not making eye contact with Derrin or her friends.

"I haven't finished my drink." She then began to take small sips. Derrin huffed. He slowly moved up behind Chloe and pressed his body against her butt. Chloe could feel his growing erection. He positioned his manhood at the crux of her butt cheeks. She nearly choked when she realized he wanted her. He leaned in close to her right ear, as she sipped the drink, and whispered, "You have approximately three minutes before I kiss you. It's your choice either right here in front of my sister and your friends or outside. What's it going to be?"

Chloe cut her eyes to Cara who was sitting on the edge of her seat as if Derrin was going to ask for a threesome with her. Diane sat slouched back in her chair like the room was spinning. But Kenya remained standing with her hands on her hips. Chloe was not sure but something told her Kenya was waiting for her to say something. Not wanting to give in to Derrin just yet, Chloe decided to compromise. She turned to Derrin and retorted.

"I will go outside with you, but if I don't like what you have to say, I *will* be returning to the game."

Derrin mumbled incoherently, *Yeah, right.*

Chloe placed her glass back on the table and asked Kenya to hand her purse over. Kenya remained silent. She simply handed Chloe the purse and rolled her eyes at Derrin who would not make eye contact with her. Chloe turned around and noticed the Twister guy was standing watching the scene unfold. He began walking toward them. In an effort to avoid a scene and to keep things low key, she began swiftly moving past Derrin in the direction of the stairs to the first level and exit door. Derrin was nearly on her heels. He placed the palm of his hand on the small of her back and gently guided her through the packed room. She wondered if he was just trying to send a signal that he was marking his territory. This thought pissed Chloe off. By the time they exited the building and reached the edge of the parking lot she was smoking mad.

Derrin grabbed hold of her hand and gently pulled her across the lot to his car. He pressed the alarm on his Acura Integra. He reached to open the passenger side door, when Chloe pushed the door closed and turned to face him. Their faces were inches apart. Chloe's attention moved from his eyes to his mouth and back to his eyes.

His baritone voice nearly echoed in the night air. "Chloe, please just get in the car." He was nearly begging her to cooperate. However, Chloe was still pissed that she felt he was making a claim to her knowing he did not want a committed relationship.

"Derrin, what was all that about? I mean you tell me how you don't want a committed relationship, but you act like I am yours. I don't get it. I was having a good time trying to give this dating thing a chance and you suddenly appeared, acting like the world was coming to an end. So, what's the deal?" Chloe crossed her arms over her chest and released a deep breath. She was fighting back the anger.

Derrin easily moved her arms apart and inched closer to her. He smoothed his hand across her bare shoulder and then glanced into her eyes.

"I'm accustomed to getting what I want, when I want it, for as long as I want it and from whomever I want it. Until I met you I could care less if a woman I was interested in flirted with another man. I would just cut her loose and keep moving on to the next one. But when I saw you smile at that guy and his feet were nearly rubbing on you like mine were when we watched the movie, I wanted to choke him. I have never been jealous over any woman not even Nicole and I was engaged to her." Chloe let out a small gasp. Derrin continued talking without moving his hand from Chloe's shoulder.

"After I realized what happened I got pissed at myself. I never wanted to do anything to embarrass you. I saw the look in your eyes when I was ordering you to put your shoes on. I did not know how to undo the damage. I just wanted to kiss you."

"Derrin, you can't kiss me whenever you need to apologize. You will have to use words as well as actions." Derrin lowered his head to Chloe's neck and planted soft wet kisses down her neck from her chin to her collarbone.

"Okay, I promise to use words AND kisses when I mess up. Now, will you get in the car?"

Chloe huffed. "We need to talk. I think you are acting this way because of the fact that I was a virgin when we slept together. This will all wear off when you get over this knight in shining armor routine because you were my first." Chloe really believed every word she said. She was proud of herself for deciphering through Derrin's issues. But before she could pat herself on the back, Derrin retorted, "You are so far from the truth. First, you are not the first virgin I have slept with and second your body makes me feel things I have never felt even with more experienced women. So this is not some novelty I will get over." He slightly kissed her lips not wanting to start something he could not finish in the parking lot. He continued, "Now, please get in the car."

Chloe was satisfied with his responses for the moment. She needed to process everything he revealed. She slipped inside of the navy blue Acura. The leather seats were soft and felt warm to the touch. Derrin rushed to the driver's side and entered the vehicle. He started the engine and pulled out of the parking lot. He glanced in the rear view mirror and promised to himself that he would not let Chloe come back here to play games with strange men.

Chloe was bobbing her head to the music on the radio. A Mary J. Blige song played in the car. She was deep in thought until Derrin muted the volume.

"Chloe it is about a twenty minute drive to my loft. I hope that is enough time for you to come up with a compromise plan for us. When we get inside, I will give you another ten minutes to explain the details then it will be the end of discussion. After that I plan to make love to you all night."

Chloe starred at him as if he was speaking Russian. She finally asked, "What is a compromise plan for us?"

"One where you and I date, spend time together, make love and enjoy each other for as long as we both agree. With both of us knowing we will not fall in love."

"Let me get it straight. Basically you want a long term no strings attached fling?"

"You can call it what you want. Just think of a list of 'must have' demands and 'would like' demands and we will hash out the details when we get to my loft."

Chloe wanted to blurt out a quick jab but she could only frown her eyebrows and tilt her head. *He must be losing his mind*, she thought. Instead of saying anything, she turned the volume knob and allowed the music to fill the space between her and Derrin.

"Chloe, you are highly intelligent and I am sure you can come up with a plan that melds my goals with yours, without love and marriage." Chloe never turned her head from starring out the passenger window.

They rode the rest of the way in silence. Chloe sat with the palms of her hands pressed flat against her capris. She nervously patted her thighs.

Her cell phone vibrated. She had a text message. It was from Kenya. The text read: "SMH@u. Told u so, play hard to get, tho." Chloe laughed. She knew Kenya's text actually meant, "I am shaking my head at you. Remember what I told you about getting Derrin, but at least pretend to make it difficult for him." She loved Kenya's straightforwardness.

Chloe contemplated Derrin's request. He was being honest with her about the type of relationship he wanted. Perhaps she shouldn't worry and just trust her heart and go with the flow. It was not like she wasn't already in love with him. Thus, there was nothing he could do to prevent something that had already happened. She needed to determine if she could handle secretly loving him knowing that he was averse to falling in love with her or any woman. Come to think of it, Chloe just recalled Derrin saying he was engaged before. She was unaware that he had taken the time to fall in love in the past. *I wonder what happened? Hmm.*

CHAPTER EIGHT

As promised, Derrin and Chloe arrived at his Alpharetta loft in less than half an hour. During the drive neither of them mumbled nor spoke a word while concentrating deeply on their respective thoughts. Chloe was seriously contemplating calling a cab and leaving as soon as she stepped foot on the parking lot asphalt. Her heart told her to give this a chance because her love for him and his desire for her would overcome the inhibitions over whether or not they would be in a committed relationship. The intelligence she worked vigorously to develop with both common sense and a college education, swayed her to evaluate how she would handle Derrin leaving her high and dry whenever he got bored with her. She continued to believe, in spite of his discourse on his relations with virgins, that her being a virgin led to his sudden desire to possess and claim her as his. He was definitely asserting his alpha male tendencies tonight with his display of sexual anger, control and assertiveness.

Deep within her soul, Chloe was overjoyed that a man as gorgeous as Derrin wanted to stake a claim to her. She watched as the other ladies at the event silently envied her as she exited with Derrin hot on her heels. The entire scene evaluated after the excitement died down was exciting more than it was embarrassing.

Chloe followed Derrin from the parking lot to the elevator bay, where he placed a special access key in the control panel and the elevator transported them to the top floor. Initially, Chloe did not suspect there was anything different about Derrin's loft, but when he opened the door and stepped aside for her to enter, she lost her breath at the magnificent view of the night sky. The loft had a retractable ceiling on the back half of the room. The entire area was open and spacious, in fact except for the bathroom areas and the partial wall dividing the kitchen and the living room, the first floor of the loft was one big room. The violet walls, lavender accent color and white baseboards in the living room gave the room a masculine yet trendy feel.

Chloe walked further into the loft and positioned herself directly under the partially open skylight. The night sky was beautiful. She was so mesmerized by the view that she was unaware of Derrin's presence until he finally spoke.

"Tonight the moon looks as if you can touch it. What do you think?" He casually inquired as if it was common place to gaze at the stars and moon right from the comfort of your living room. Chloe was speechless. She did not respond instead she just starred upward at the sky. She was inwardly trying to determine if she was ready for their conversation to start or be over. She quickly learned that time was not her friend. Derrin was removing his shoes and pulling his shirt tail from his pants, Chloe could tell he wanted to put his plans in action sooner rather than later.

Chloe huffed and looked at Derrin. When their eyes met, he stopped moving. Her eyes roamed across his entire face but she refused to look past his chin. In spite of wanting to appreciate his entire body especially his smooth muscular chest, Chloe needed to study his demeanor and reaction to her suggestions.

She moved to place her purse on the kitchen bar stool then she removed her stiletto sandals.

"Hmm. Derrin, are you sure you want to do this?" Her voice was shaking as she attempted to conceal her plea for them to stop the direction things were going between them. He put his hands in his pockets and leaned against the edge of the counter.

"I am as sure as I know my name is what it is. Chloe, I want you.

So, if I have to break my rules to get you then I will. I know you are hesitant about this that's why we need to talk first," he crossed his legs at the ankles and braced himself for her retort.

She began, "Ideally, what I want from a relationship is to know I am special, to have the comfort in knowing I am the only one and that I am building something that could springboard into forever. You on the other hand want just the opposite. Simply put, you merely want to control the person you have sexual relations with. I am not ready for that type of relationship."

Derrin's heart was pounding so hard in his chest he thought she could see his shirt moving with each beat. Finally, he responded, "I don't want to control you. I just don't want to share you."

She responded, "Being monogamous is not a problem for me, but will it be an issue for you? You are the one who changes women whenever you flip the calendar month. Can you commit to being with me and only me until we decide it's time to move on?"

Chloe waited with baited breath. Her decision hinged on his reply to this simple question.

"All I have to say is – absolutely. Chloe, you don't seem to understand that I have no problem being exclusive because you are the only person I want now. When that changes we will alter our interaction and amicably end things." Derrin removed his hands from his pockets and uncrossed his legs, silently hoping and anticipating she would come to him.

He was highly disappointed when instead of moving closer to him, Chloe actually retreated. She glided over to the glass patio door which led to the balcony. Other than her bare feet touching the floor with each step, the room was silent. Chloe opened the door and stepped out into the brisk April air. She closed the door behind her leaving Derrin alone in his kitchen.

I need air. I need to think. Chloe thought as she tried to process Derrin's appeal.

Derrin released the breath he had been holding and decided he needed to calm his nerves. He could understand Chloe's hesitation, but most women would jump at the chance to be in an exclusive relationship with him. There lied his problem. Chloe was not just any woman. She was intelligent, gorgeous, self sufficient and independent. She was the polar opposite of the women he had dated in the past five years. In fact, she did not actually need him for anything, well maybe for a good roll in the hay. Derrin poured himself a shot of bourbon to help his mind deal with the possibility of rejection. Until now it never occurred to him that Chloe would really deny his request. He rarely had women deny him anything.

As he threw back a second shot, he thought *Man, chalk up your losses and keep your pride intact.* He turned to walk toward the balcony where he planned to join Chloe, when she slid the door opened and stepped back into the room.

Her eyes revealed her decision long before her lips ever did. Derrin saw through the depths of her soul and knew she would agree to the arrangement.

"Derrin, you have to know that this decision is hard for me because I have already broken the rules," she blurted out when she was fully standing back in the room. He frowned his eyebrows and squinted his eyes not understanding where she was going with this declaration.

"Let me finish. You want us to be in an exclusive affair with neither of us falling in love with the other. Well..., I must confess ... that I am ... already in love with you, which means the only thing I can expect from you is for you to be honest when you want to leave. I don't want you to play me for a fool." She finally allowed her breathing to slow down. He simply nodded his agreement.

His urgency to take her in his arms and kiss her, taste her, be with her flooded his thoughts. He slammed the shot glass down on the counter and swept her up in his arms.

Derrin reached out for Chloe and pulled her into his arms. His lips were hot and wet. They naturally molded to her lips. She sighed and parted her lips. Derrin eased his tongue into her mouth and began to lick and flick around her tongue. His lips slowly sucked her lips causing Chloe to throw her head back and groan. Her groans triggered Derrin's all out assault on her mouth. He could not get enough. As he moved forward, Chloe moved backwards. They never parted. Eventually, she was pressed against the banister to the stairs. When her back touched the wood rail she opened her eyes. Derrin was staring back at her. He pulled back and slightly kissed her lips again before he picked Chloe up and carried her up the stairs. The journey up the ten stairs seemed to take forever, because Chloe's body was tingling in places she did not know could tingle. She wanted to rip her clothes off in hopes that the cool air would lower her body temperature. But she knew as long as Derrin was holding her she would always be hot for him.

Derrin placed Chloe on the bed while his eyes roamed from her face to her toes. He slowly licked his lips.

"Chloe, I want you. I plan to adore you and never hurt you. Rest assured I won't play you for a fool."

She closed her eyes and slowly opened her mouth to speak. "I want you too, Derrin. I'm ready to get this, to get "us" started. Please make love to me."

Derrin smiled deviously. He reached for the clasp of her Capri pants and unbuttoned them and gradually slid them down her legs. Chloe raised her butt a little to make the removal easier. Derrin then slipped her pink lace panties down her leg. Once he removed them he tossed them over his shoulder to the floor. Chloe giggled.

Derrin leaned down and planted kisses on her thighs then he kissed her stomach. But it was the licks on her belly button and sides of her stomach that made Chloe bounce up from the bed and grab him around the neck. Their lips met and the kisses were more passionate than before. Chloe's hunger for Derrin resembled a lion conquering his competition. She used her lips to kiss, suck and make love to Derrin's mouth. She was daring and unashamed. She planned to enjoy every second of being with Derrin. As she devoured his mouth and lips, Chloe's body was awakened by Derrin's hands and fingers.

Derrin was relentless in his pursuit of pleasing her. Chloe enjoyed the way he used his thumb and forefinger to caress her nipples until they perked up and pointed at him. She also admired the tender way he touched her waist and thighs. With each flick of his tongue, suck of his lips and caress of his hands, Chloe became more and more sexually aroused. She wanted Derrin and he very well knew it. Derrin paused and stared at Chloe briefly, before he retrieved a condom packet from his nightstand.

"As you can see I am prepared this time. I want you to enjoy every moment without any worries." Derrin said as he rolled the condom down his shaft.

"Derrin, I was not worried the first time."

He glanced up and made direct eye contact with Chloe to express the seriousness of his next statement.

"Neither was I. For the record, if you were pregnant, I would have been proud to be the father of your child."

Chloe rose up from the bed and planted a wet, hot kiss on his lips.

"Thank you. Now, that's enough talking." He whispered before he continued his lustful assault on her senses.

Derrin glided the tips of his fingers lightly down Chloe's cheek, continuing across her shoulder, over her breast, pausing briefly to manipulate her nipples to arousal, finally passing down her stomach to the area between her legs. Chloe was on edge by the time he reached his destination. She wanted him more than she had ever wanted anything in her life. She closed her eyes to shut out her environment and focus completely on the sexual pleasure she was experiencing.

Derrin lowered his head and flicked his tongue across the same path as his fingertips had taken. Chloe was wired to explode. As he utilized his fingers and tongue to push her over the edge, she spread her legs to allow him full access to her. She pushed her bottom up and leaned back to give herself to him. She moaned continuously from the pleasure each touch and sensation brought her. She could not contain herself any longer. "Derrin, please. Now, I need you to be a part of me."

Derrin did not say one word. He merely lowered his mouth to the area between her thighs and made love with his tongue until her legs trembled. She collapsed on the bed. He smiled. Finally, he positioned himself over her and entered her. She groaned with pleasure and slowly gyrated and thrust toward him. With each move she could feel him. The pleasure he evoked made her cry. Their lovemaking was cyclical, they climaxed, slept, woke up and started again. Ultimately they fell asleep from exhaustion.

Chloe curled up in front of him, closed her eyes and drifted off to sleep with a smile on her face. She lay naked in the bed next to the man she had been fascinated with for nearly eight years. She could not imagine any better way to fall asleep.

The morning sun began to move from behind the clouds and shine through the windows. Derrin moved closer to Chloe. He found he could not get enough of her touch or smell, he assumed it was his infatuation with Chloe that was the reason he begged her for this relationship. Yes, he called it a fling but he knew it was a relationship, the very thing he dreaded. He was lost in his thoughts when the phone began to ring. The caller ID told him it was his sister. Chloe wiggled and gradually opened her eyes. The look on her face gave him the impression that she was concerned he was not answering the phone. He suspected she thought it was a woman he did not want to talk to with her in his bed. He wanted to reassure her, but she swiftly jumped from the bed grabbed her shirt and went to the bathroom.

He decided to go ahead and answer the phone because Kenya was not going to stop calling and the more the phone rang the more Chloe would doubt his commitment to their relationship. He picked up the receiver and listened to Kenya blast his ears off in her tirade about last night. He heard the water in the bathroom sink stop and knew he needed to end this madness before Chloe came out of the bathroom.

"Good bye, Kenya. I will tell her, now go do something. We are busy over here." Derrin laughed as his sister began to spew obscenities at him while he placed the phone on the cradle.

He glanced toward the master bathroom and peered over at Chloe standing leaning against the doorjamb with nothing but her burgundy one armed shirt on. *God, she is beautiful.* Derrin thought.

"Ken wants you to call her and let her know you are safe and not being held over here against your will by some crazed man who just happens to be her older brother. She is all freaked out about what happened last night." Derrin rolled over and curled his arms around the pillow. His senses reacted to Chloe's scent on his pillows and sheets and on him. He smiled as his erection grew.

Chloe did not move, she continued to lean against the door and look at him. From her body language, Derrin knew she was pondering something. He also knew it was something either about him or their new arrangement.

Chloe finally pushed off the door, put her arms behind her back and tilted her head before she opened her mouth. "Hmm", she pondered. "Who is she, Derrin?" Derrin closed his eyes and did not respond. He knew this part of their conversation was going to come up sooner or later, but he was hoping it would have been later rather than sooner. He did not want to respond.

Chloe continued, "I want to know about the woman who has your heart and has not returned it. She must have been a masterpiece to get you give up your heart in the first place. Now that she is gone and left the devastation in her wake, I want to know what happened. No, I need to know what happened or this 'exclusive fling' we are starting will be a colossal disaster." Derrin opened his eyes and patted the mattress. He wanted Chloe to sit down beside him when he discussed Nicole. The thought of talking about Nicole made him want to vomit.

Chloe obliged and sat on the edge of the bed, she wanted to be far enough away that she would not succumb to his tempting touches.

"First, Nicole does not still have my heart. I snatched it back and locked it up after we broke up. She was someone who I believed I wanted to share my life with. I thought she represented the wife, mother and soulmate that I wanted. I hoped she would be the woman for me like my mother was to my father. I believed it would be until death do us part. Well, since in the end I wanted to kill her, I guess she did represent the principle of death do us part." He smirked at his own comment. "Anyway, she was a deceiver. She made me believe she was one person when in actuality she was another. The Nicole I fell in love with did not exist. She was trained in seducing and convincing men to think of her as this person who cared about them, their hopes and desires."

Derrin paused and rolled over onto his back. He stared at the ceiling for a few moments. Then he continued, "You know she was like the Geisha girls, who convince the customer they are one person when in reality they are just working." Every muscle in her body had tensed as she listened to Derrin describe his ex-fiancé Nicole. The pain resonated through each word he spoke.

"I'm sorry you fell for the deception. But you have to know you can't keep your heart locked up forever. If you do you will never be happy. And this thing we are agreeing to won't bring you happiness either." She was calm and straightforward.

"I know. But until I am ready to deal with all of it, I can't unlock my heart for any woman, not even one as trustworthy and beautiful as you, Chloe."

"Derrin, I have only two more questions, then this conversation will be over. Question number one: Who ended the relationship you or her? And question number two: Do you still love what she represented?" Chloe was fighting to hold down her emotions which were getting the best of her. She had uncontrolled anxiety in anticipation of his reply.

"She ended the relationship when she thought her new dude could provide for her better than I could," he replied then paused. He continued, "I don't know if I love what she represented or not. I am not in love with her, but beneath all my anger I think I still care for her in a friend kind of way." He rubbed his milk chocolate colored hands down his face and sighed. After this discussion, he hoped Chloe would not take off running out the front door. Instead, she leaned in close to him and kissed him. He was elated.

"You, Chloe Dancy are more than I bargained for," he said in a deep raspy tone that sounded more intimate with each syllable he spoke.

"Is being more than you bargained for a good thing or a bad thing?" she inquired.

He leaned up toward her mouth and pulled her down on the bed. "I can show you better than I can tell you," he whispered.

His touch sent varied sensations through Chloe's body. She took a sharp intake of air when he brushed his tongue against her lips and flicked his tongue against hers. Each time he was more provocative than the last. He used slow detailed movements to excite her passion. He stirred her desires to the fullest with his mouth. Before long he pulled her shirt over her head and tossed it across the room. His hands cupped her breasts and he flicked his fingers over her hardened nipples. They instantly responded and drew into elongated buds. She impatiently waited for his mouth to taste and touch her. Derrin was not going to be rushed. Last night he let his desire overwhelm him and force him to ravage her to quench his thirst. Today he planned to take his time and learn what excited her body and determine the spots where he could torture her into a sexual abyss. His mouth and hands were on her breasts immediately, lightly cupping and caressing one while his mouth greedily devoured the other. He was absorbing everything about her, her taste, her essence, her seduction. He believed she was the cause for the emotional havoc going on in his mind and heart.

She was like a meal he just had to consume. He wanted all of her. He wanted to do more than whet his appetite. He rolled Chloe over on the bed and slowly glided his hands down her abdomen sending tantalizing chills through her spine. While his mouth continued its assault on her lips, his fingers explored her feminine essence. She was wet, slippery and ready for him. He did not want her to wait any longer. He gripped her hips and moved his knees to spread her thighs apart. He entered her with ease as a flood of emotions coursed through her body. She cried out his name. Frissons of pleasure oozed from every cell in her body before she was able to brace herself for the onslaught of orgasmic tremors. Derrin was satisfied by the pleasure he brought her. The more he wanted to satisfy her, the deeper he thrust. Finally he reached a climax and collapsed, spent from the experience. He repositioned his body to lie on his stomach with his arms stretched across the bed. Chloe watched as the birds and clouds moved across the sky above.

The clock on the nightstand told her it was past noon on Saturday, but her stomach told her she was hungry. She decided to rise and take inventory of the food available in the cupboards. She carefully walked down the stairs making every effort not to awake Derrin. She reached the landing and moved swiftly and effortlessly to the kitchen.

Other than five different types of juices and dozens of sodas and condiments, the refrigerator was nearly bare. She was fortunate to find a few eggs, a pack of cheese, onions and tomatoes. With these ingredients she could work some magic and make an omelet or two. She started the coffee brewer and began her effort to feed herself and Derrin. She paused at the thought that she was actually cooking for a man. She wanted everything to be perfect in spite of the sparse nature of the meal. After she prepared the omelets she put a few pieces of bread in the toaster. As she was placing the diced tomatoes and shredded cheese across the top of the omelets, Derrin walked up behind her and kissed her on the neck. She nearly jumped out of her skin. She was pleasantly surprised.

"Good morning, sexy," he said as he continued to kiss her neck. Before she responded, Chloe titled her head further to the side to allow him easy access.

"It was a good morning, now it is a good afternoon since it is almost twelve thirty. You should be hungry after your morning activities." She watched him kiss her shoulder. "I hope you like eggs because that is all I could find to cook. What do you do for food around here?" She asked.

"I eat out. I don't get in until late in the evening so I stop to eat on the way home. Plus, I hate washing dishes." He moved his hands up and down the sides of her waist. He wanted to tell her that he was hungry for her, but the smell of the food permeated his thoughts and he decided it would be a good idea to eat.

"I love eggs. I'm sure yours are the best." He continued and moved to pick up one of the plates Chloe had fixed with omelets, toast and jelly. Chloe followed him around the island to the high boy stools. As she walked around him to sit, she noticed a picture hanging in his living room area. It was simply gorgeous. The picture depicted a lady wearing a purple dress with a lavender scarf blowing in the wind toward the left of the scene. At the lady's knees a little boy was tightly clinging to her body crying. The inscription read: *Love can heal all pain.*

She walked closer to get a better view. Derrin turned on the stool and watched Chloe's reaction. Chloe inched closer to the point where her face was nearly touching the glass in the frame. Then it dawned on her that this was not a picture or a painting, it was a large cross-stitch. She twisted around to stare at Derrin. He was watching her and eating eggs, silently.

"Derrin is this one of your cross-stitches?" Her eyes grew wider in anticipation of his answer.

"Yes. It took me and Mom nearly six months to complete it." He was proud of his masterpiece as evidenced by the bright gleam on his face when he responded.

"I'm speechless." Chloe with her mouth open walked back toward the island where Derrin was sitting.

Derrin patted the high boy stool implying that he wanted her to sit down. He then added, "Come sit and I will tell you the story." Chloe obliged him.

Derrin began telling Chloe how his mother was upset that he was mean and bitter after his broken engagement. His mother felt that she was losing him to anger, so she had the grandson of one of her church friends take a box of family photos. The grandson was supposed to create a blueprint of a photo in the box so his mother could use it as a cross stitch pattern. What his mother did not know was that the boy was a graphic arts and computer engineering major in college.

He sifted through all the photos and decided to meld three separate pictures together to form the design. The first picture was one of Derrin crying after he fell off his bike when he was five years old. The next two were of his mother on a mountain when she was younger. The boy pasted the pictures together, enlarged the scenes to remove their feet and the background scenery. He made a computer image and placed it on a cross-stitch grid. When his grandmother gave it to Derrin's mother, she cried. He and his mother used the time cross-stitching the picture to talk about his anger and Nicole. After they finished the cross-stitch, he assumed his mother would keep it. Instead, she added the inscription and had it framed for his loft when she decorated it.

A single tear ran down Chloe's cheek. She could not believe the history of the picture. She did not know what to say. He wiped the wet streak on her face.

"Oh, Derrin. That is so beautiful. Was the inscription her way of showing you that if you give love a try it can heal your heart?"

Derrin looked back at the picture not wanting to acknowledge that his mother made that same comment to him when she hung the picture on the wall.

He shrugged his shoulders and replied, "I like my interpretation better. I think the picture depicts the depths of a mother's love for her son when he is scared and hurting. It has nothing to do with any other kind of love."

Chloe lightly laughed. She realized Derrin was hell bent on not seeing love for what it was. She leaned in toward him, placed her hands flat on his thighs and kissed him.

"Well, I think it is beautiful and is perfect for your home." Chloe concluded. Derrin initiated another kiss and stood from the stool. He picked up the plates to put them in the dishwasher.

"I need to take you home to get your car. So, get dressed." He said matter-of-factly without hesitation.

"Get my car? Why would I need to get my car if you take me home? Duh." Chloe thumped her fingers at Derrin as if he made a mistake. He crossed his eyes and turned completely around.

"Like I said I need to take you home to get your car. Either that or you will have to drive my car to work on Monday morning because you are staying here with me all weekend. If you want to stay without clean clothes and other necessities, that's fine with me."

She took a few deep breaths and tried to process his statements. She had never stayed overnight with a man let alone an entire weekend. This new arrangement was definitely going to be an eye opener. But she was inwardly flipping with excitement at the thought that she would be with Derrin enjoying his company and he hers.

CHAPTER NINE

C hloe could not believe the entire weekend went by so quickly. She vaguely remembered going to her house to get a few things and returning to Derrin's loft. She stopped by the local grocery store on her way back to pick up a few items to cook for them. They did not leave the loft other than to go Applebee's Sunday evening for dinner. She enjoyed watching the Sunday morning talking heads with Derrin and discussing their views on politics and the economy. She laughed when he did impersonations of the President of the United States and his sidekick the goofy Vice President. She read the newspaper with him and noticed he has a pet peeve when the sections are not placed back in order after someone read them. Most notable, she enjoyed making love with him and falling asleep curled up beside him. She dreaded the beginning of the work week when she had to leave this haven.

Chloe and Derrin showered together when he returned from his daily run. She hot curled her hair in the bathroom while he brushed his teeth. As she watched him through the wall mirror above the sink, she cringed. She knew she would end up moving from having a simple crush on Derrin to having a full blown love affair. She also knew this would not bode well for her heart when he wanted to end things. He left the small space and went to get dressed and read the newspaper downstairs. She continued to get dressed in her black tailored pants suit. The jacket was form fitting around her waist and flared out above her hips. Her three inch open toe silver heels were coordinated to match the large silver embellishments which served as buttons on the jacket. The pants were hip hugging and drew attention to her firm round butt.

Derrin was downstairs dressed in a logo tee shirt for his store Café Coffee and a pair of khaki pants, which was dressy for his line of work. He was glad he did not have to wear business suits and ties anymore. He easily grew tired of the business attire rules. He grabbed his keys and was waiting on Chloe before he left. When she descended the stairs with her overnight bag, briefcase and purse, he rushed to help her. Once he placed the overnight bag and briefcase on the floor, he glanced up and inspected her outfit.

"You are a tad bit too sexy for an architectural firm aren't you, missy?" he chided.

Chloe spun around on her toes and rubbed her hands down her hips. "What? This is just a regular black suit." She retorted.

"No, ma'am it is not. Make this the last day you wear that suit to work. I won't be able to concentrate today knowing your male co-workers will be staring at your butt all day." He had walked up and grabbed her butt as he talked. He lightly squeezed for emphasis when he was finished speaking.

Chloe felt flush. *Is he for real? No way.* She thought to herself.

"You are tripping. My co-workers have not noticed anything about me that would be sexy. Trust me, I know." She felt as though this was more of a confession that a reply.

Derrin raised his eyebrows. The slip did not get past him.

"Chloe Dancy, do you have the hots for one of your co-workers?" he inquired. She did not respond with words, she merely rolled her eyes. He continued, "You don't seem to believe that you are sexy, but you are and I know you have the men drooling even if they are not acting on their lust." He tilted his head and kissed her. His tongue was beginning to believe it belonged in her mouth more than in his own. He could not get enough of her, but he knew he had to stop this before he took her back upstairs and made her late for work. He pulled back from her.

"Like I said make this the last time you wear these pants hugging my butt like this." He grinned.

Chloe laughed and inquired, "Your butt? Don't you mean my butt?" He answered, "No, I meant my butt. Now, let's go so you aren't late." He kissed the tip of her nose and opened the front door. They exited and rode the elevator to the parking garage. Derrin placed her overnight bag in the trunk and put her briefcase on the front passenger floor. He pulled her toward him one last time and hugged her close.

"See you later," he said as if it was guaranteed.

"Okay." Chloe then opened the driver's side door and got in her gold Lexus SUV truck.

After she pulled out of the parking garage and stopped at the first red light she pinched herself to make sure it was all real.

Chloe decided it was time to call Kenya and tell her about the arrangement she has with Derrin. She dreaded Kenya's reaction, which is why she exerted great effort to press the numbers as slowly as possible.

Kenya answered the call and sucked her teeth into the receiver with such skill that Chloe could fully envision how her best friend looked as she made the noise signifying her annoyance.

"Hey, girl. What's up?" Chloe began.

"Oh, nothing. I was just sitting here wondering when my best friend planned to resurface or if she planned to stay holed up with the madman commonly known as my brother." Kenya responded tartly even though she was not as pissed with Chloe as she pretended to be.

"Well, you will be happy to know that your best friend is on her way to work and is no longer enjoying the company of your handsome gorgeous yet demanding brother." Chloe said as her lips smoothly glided into a wide smile.

"Demanding? That's an understatement. From his reaction to you playing Twister and footsies with Russ I would conclude he is a little more than demanding. But enough about what I think, what is he demanding that you do?"

"Uh, I shouldn't have said he was demanding maybe that term is too harsh. He is persistent. When he knows what he wants he intends to get it." Chloe's mind drifted off as she spoke these words.

"Chloe you have exactly thirty seconds to tell me what is going on or I am going to hang up this phone and come to your job to shake it out of you." Kenya informed her.

"Well, it seems that your lovely brother was so jealous of seeing me laughing and touching another man that he decided we needed to have a committed affair. I reluctantly agreed with two conditions."

"Hold up. You have said way too much for me to grasp it all. Are you telling me that you and Derrin are having a fling?"

"You make it sound so trashy. It really is more than a fling. It is a pseudo relationship."

Kenya burst out laughing before she continued her inquiry.

"Okay. So you and Derrin have a faux relationship. But what are the two conditions?"

Chloe bit her lip before she began. She was contemplating the right words to use to explain things. She thought it would be best to just get it out and deal with Kenya's reaction later.

"First, we both agreed to be exclusive and second, if either of us becomes tired of the other we will just say it and move on with no hard feelings or strings attached. Of course, we are not supposed to fall in love or expect the other to fall in love, but that is a minor hiccup since I told him I was already in love with him."

"I changed my mind," Kenya snapped. "I am going to come to your job and shake you but now just on principle. What in the world were you thinking when you agreed to this mess? Derrin is a big wuss. He is scared to fall in love and now he has convinced you to buy into his foolishness." Kenya paused before she continued. "Yeah, I need to shake you."

Chloe giggled at the thought. Chloe knew Kenya had her best interests at heart. She did not want to belabor the point for fear that Kenya just might come to her job and shake some sense into her.

"Ken I will be fine. I know Derrin is not going to fall in love with me and for now that is okay. When I want more I will leave this relationship and find my husband. Until then, I'm good."

"Okay... but remember that you are worthy of more from a man especially one like Derrin, who can give you more than you ever imagined. You just can't let him put you in a box. Think about that." Kenya smiled. She loved her friend and wanted the best for her. Then she recalled she had not caught her up on the activities from the weekend.

"Girl, enough about you and Derrin. Guess who Cara went home with from the event Friday night?" Kenya excitedly questioned.

Chloe tried to think but no one came to mind. She presumed it must have been an ex-boyfriend. "I have no idea, knowing Cara it could have been the DJ and the bartender. Just tell me." Chloe's comment made her and Kenya both chuckle.

"No, not the DJ or bartender, but Russ. You know, the guy who sent my brother over the edge. I called her Saturday morning and she was breathing hard like she just came from an aerobics class. She said she would call me back when he left, but I have not heard from her."

"Get out!" Chloe exclaimed then her chuckle progressed into a full blown laugh. She imagined Cara's reaction to Russ' high pitched voice in the heat of passion and could not suppress her laugh. Chloe continued laughing as she pulled into her employer's parking lot and found a parking space. She wiped the tears from her eyes.

"I can't wait to talk to Cara. I am sure she has a story to tell about her weekend." Chloe grabbed her purse and opened the car door. "Ken I am at the office now. I will have to call you later." Chloe softly responded.

"I will talk to you later." Kenya disconnected the call and debated calling Derrin but she quickly decided against it.

The work day passed quickly for Chloe. She was working on a project for a very influential client which required her full attention. She attempted to concentrate on designing the floor plans for the first floor of the new building the client contracted her to design. There were times when she would think of Derrin in the middle of the creating the plans. Whenever she imagined hardwood floors she thought of Derrin's loft which caused her thoughts to drift to his bed and what they did there. When she was sketching the conference rooms and thought of the glass walls she added to the designs her thoughts strolled to the memory of Derrin kissing her in the family room with the skylight open. She figured nothing could top that view.

Chloe stopped working on the designs. She sat back in her chair and smiled. Her stomach fluttered at thoughts of Derrin and their lovemaking. She would never have imagined that she would be the object of his desire. *Me and Derrin, who would have thought it was possible? Not in a million years.*

Chloe was drawn out of her day dream when the phone began to ring. She could tell from the double ring that the call was from someone outside of the company. She glanced at the Caller Id screen and did not recognize the number.

"Good morning. Chloe Dancy. How may I help you?" She half heartedly said when she answered the call.

"Actually it's no longer morning." The baritone voice made the cells in her body tingle. She knew instantly it was Derrin.

"You are so correct. It is now afternoon. How may I help you Mr. Reynolds?" Chloe teased.

"You can help me by agreeing to come over tonight. I want to see you and I need to hold you, kiss you. What do you say?"

"Ah, that is so sweet. But I have a deadline to get the floor plans designed for the first floor of a client's new commercial building. I have to finish most of it before I leave tonight. Can I have a rain check?" The disappointment filled Chloe's voice.

"Hmm. I guess I can postpone my plans for another night or so. But I am not one who takes rejection well." Derrin smiled brightly as he envisioned Chloe's face.

"You have a deal. I think I will have this part of the designs finished by tomorrow so I can come over then. That is if the offer is still open." For some reason Chloe held her breath wondering if Derrin would change his mind.

"Chloe, let's not go there. Of course, the offer will still be open tomorrow, the next day, the day after that and so on until we decide this thing we have has run its course. And I don't imagine that will be anytime soon." Derrin spoke dryly and calmly.

Chloe paused before responding. "Okay. I'll see you tomorrow."

After a brief moment of silence, Derrin chimed in.

"Well, it's a date. I'll call you tomorrow. Kisses." He made a kissing sound and laughed, then hung up the phone.

Chloe decided, after several painstaking minutes of thought that she would refrain from making comments which showed her lack of faith in their arrangement. She truly believed Derrin was a man of his word and when he wanted out he would let her know. Until then she would just go with the flow.

The remainder of the afternoon proceeded at a quicker pace. She found the wherewithal to complete the floor plans with the exception of a few small aesthetic characteristics. She decided to finalize those features tomorrow. She went without lunch and was really ready to get home to kick back and relax.

She left the office and stopped by the local seafood market to pick up some steamed crawfish and shrimp. She planned to prepare corn and potatoes to go along with her seafood. Once she purchased her items she went to her Lexus parked in the front of the store. She pushed her door release button on the key fob and mindlessly walked to the driver's side of the vehicle. Then her eyes met those of a stray dog. She froze. She could not move, all she could do was stare at the dingy white dog with matted clumps of hair and one ear.

She tried to convince herself that the small dog would not harm her. She moved her right foot forward so she could open the car door. In the process, she dropped the bag and a few steamed crawfish fell out of the bag. The dog smelled the food and began growling. He showed his yellow teeth and Chloe screamed. She ran away from the car as fast as her heels would take her. She kicked the crawfish accidently as she ran, causing the dog to follow on her trail.

With each step she screamed and the dog barked. They ran clear across the parking lot into the driveway for a nearby church. Chloe reached out and grabbed the doors but they were locked. She thought all she could do now would be to pray that the dog did not eat her alive.

She stopped and yelled "Jesus, help me!"

At that point, an elderly man was coming from the side of the church. He saw the dog and Chloe. He realized that the Chloe was scared of the dog. He whistled and clapped his hands then the dog ran away. Chloe slid down to the ground and cried.

By the time the man reached her, she was trembling and shaking. She reached for her phone and dialed Derrin. She needed to hear his voice. She pressed the buttons and Derrin answered. She tried to speak but no sound came out of her mouth. She looked up at the elderly man and he noticed she was unable to speak. He gently grabbed the phone and placed it to his ear.

"Hello?" The man asked Derrin.

"Who is this and what happened to Chloe?" Derrin barked.

"Young man, I think this lady has just had the bejesus scared out of her. She can't talk."

"What are you talking about? Where is she?" Derrin was spitting out questions at rapid speed.

"Well, we are at Antioch Missionary Baptist Church where C.D. Thompson is our pastor. We are located at the corner of Melrose Trail and Hinton Highway." The elderly man sincerely announced as if Derrin was trying to come to the church for a revival service.

"Sir, thank you for the information. I have not heard of your church, but I know the area. Will you please ask Chloe if she needs me to come or if she can drive herself home?" Derrin was calmer now.

The elderly man looked around and noticed there were no other cars in the parking lot. "She probably can drive herself home if she had a car. But as far as I can tell she ran here when the dog was chasing her. Maybe she ran from her car." The man was rambling now as he tried to figure out where Chloe originated from before she landed on the church steps.

Chloe noticed how perplexed the old man was as he glanced around the premises. She garnered the courage to stand up. She still held her purse tightly. She brushed off her pants and rearranged her feet in her shoes.

"Thank you sir. You saved my life." Chloe expressed as she pulled the phone from his hand. She turned her head and spoke into the phone. "Hey Derrin. I'm okay now. I just had a small mishap with a stray dog. I'm fine."

"Are you sure? I got the impression that you couldn't talk when you called. Where is your car? I should come get you." Derrin was getting antsy as the possibilities ran through his head.

"My car is next door at the seafood market. I can drive myself home. I don't think it's necessary for you to worry about me. The dog is gone now." Chloe began walking toward the parking lot next door where her car was parked.

"Okay, if you say so. But please call me when you get home." Derrin pleaded.

"I promise." Chloe ended the call. She reached her car and scanned the parking lot for her furry friend. He was not in sight. She jumped in the car and sped out of the parking lot. She reached her house in record time. She pressed the garage door opener and entered. She sat in the car and took several deep breaths before she exited the car.

I'm safe at home. Chloe thought.

The remainder of the evening was a blur. She showered, ate and fell asleep on the sofa until after midnight. She relocated to her bed and caught up on her sleep.

The next day she remembered she did not call Derrin. She called him but his answering machine picked up after three rings. She left a message apologizing for not calling him back and told him that she hoped to see him later. She tried to assure him she was doing okay.

She left and went to work hoping she could complete the floor plans and leave on time for her date with Derrin. Chloe got her wish. She finished the plans at the end of her work day and walked to her boss' office to drop them off before she left for the day.

"Mr. Walker, I finished the Newvella Building 1800 first floor specs. I have them for your review." Chloe said to her boss as she handed him the disk and hard copy of the plans.

"Thank you Chloe. I was meaning to talk to you about something. Come in and have a seat."

He began, "As you know the Newvella project is one that will take nearly three years to complete. The client loves your work and wants to make sure you stay at the forefront of the project."

"I'm glad to hear that, sir. Is there anything else I should do to secure their continued support?" Chloe inquired.

"In fact there is something. The CEO has asked if you would be willing to relocate to their office in Dahlonega to oversee the plans and progress." Mr. Walker beamed with excitement as he shared the news.

Chloe tried to bite her tongue to prevent her initial reaction from coming out of her mouth. There was no way she was going to move to Dahlonega, a small town nearly fifty miles from her home. She also knew that she was not keen on leaving her proximity to downtown Atlanta, shopping areas and cultural events and places. Certainly she would not want to find a husband in the north mountain town or raise her children there, which would be a possibility since the project was going to take nearly three years to complete.

"Uh, I am not sure I could commit to moving that far from my mother. I'm an only child and she has a few medical conditions that I help monitor. Unfortunately, I am not in a position to relocate at this time." Chloe slowly declined the offer, but she thought against alienating herself from this client. She continued, "The most I can offer is to reconsider the offer within the next three months." She ended this statement with a smile, a faux smile. She backed up toward the door and began her exit.

"Chloe, I need you to keep this client. Please give this offer more thought. Let's talk again in a week." His baritone voice deepened as if he was giving a directive instead of making a request.

"Yes, we can talk in a week. I have to go, I am late for an appointment." With this Chloe turned and scurried down the hall and out to the parking lot. By the time she got inside her car, her hands were shaking. She needed her job but she was not going to move to a city where she would be so far from her family and friends. She decided to call a headhunter to help her find a new job. The thought of leaving the architectural company she had been employed with since she graduated from college made her want to cry. She steadied her hands and blinked away the tears.

When she arrived at home, she had just enough time to shower and change her clothes before Derrin rang the doorbell. The shower helped to wash away the dread of searching for a new job, but she still was a little down in the dumps.

She smoothed her Spelman t-shirt over her jeans and opened the door.

"Hi, Derrin. Come in." She moved away from the entryway and

Derrin stepped in. A smile lit his lips as delight twitched across his body. He looked her up and down appraising her from head to toe. He liked what he saw. He licked his lips as if he was glancing down on a plate of pork ribs hot off the grill.

Chloe blushed at the interaction.

"Hello to you too," Derrin said as he leaned in and kissed her lightly on the lips. He then moved to the den area. He pulled out a video from his jacket pocket and waved it in the air. "I figured you did not want to go out after the long week you are having with project deadlines. I thought you would want to curl up and watch a chick flick." He smiled. "I picked up the newest Tyler Perry movie. I believe I can stomach seeing a man in a dress for about two hours."

Chloe grinned. "If you add a massage to go with the movie, I think I too will be able to give up two hours of my day." They both laughed.

"Can I pick the body area for the massage?" Derrin asked. Chloe could only imagine what he had in mind for her massage. She raised an eyebrow and nodded.

"One massage coming up. Come over here and sit down." Derrin said before he started the video. He stood beside the sofa and rubbed his hands. He looked around before he asked Chloe for a water basin, Epsom salt and nail polish. Chloe retrieved the items and sat crossed legged on the sofa to watch as Derrin filled the basin with warm water and Epsom salt. After he had the water at the right temperature he placed the basin on a towel by the sofa. He sat down next to Chloe and slowly pulled her legs from under her bottom. Chloe lay with her back on the arm on sofa.

He began to rub the soles of her feet then he moved up to her ankles. She closed her eyes to enjoy each moment. He continued rubbing her feet and pushing her pressure points. He finally ended by wiggling each of her toes. He placed her foot in the water basin and moved to her other foot and gave it the same attention. When he finished with the second foot, he patted her soaked feet with a towel and began to put hot pink polish on her toes. She giggled and grinned at the sight of him trying to keep the polish off the sides of her toes. He blew air on each toe to get them to dry. Derrin placed her newly polished feet in his lap. Once he finished he turned his attention to the movie, but this did not last more than thirty minutes.

Derrin could not take being this close to Chloe without touching, teasing and tasting her. He glanced at her and she was biting her bottom lip. It was erotic. He knew she was not paying any attention to the movie, so he began his seduction.

He lifted one of her feet and pulled her toward him. He began sucking her toes, starting with her pinkie toe and working his way to her big toe. Each suck of her toes and flick of his tongue made her moan in anticipation. His movements were causing tingling sensations in the area between her thighs. Her nipples were perked. She was getting wetter with each suck. Chloe, with an urgency that she has never experienced before, pulled her shirt over her head to reveal her breasts. Derrin enjoyed seeing the reaction he was causing.

He moved from her toes up her ankles to her legs, but it was her thighs that he wanted to taste next. He pulled her black leggings down and noticed she was not wearing any panties, yet again. He smiled.

His warm lips and moist tongue were causing electrified sensations with each kiss and touch on her thighs. He adjusted himself and hovered over her. He planned to spend as much time as necessary pleasing her. As he moved from one thigh to the other, she gradually spread her legs. His face was eye level with her womanly core. His eyes met hers and she was just as entranced with him as he was with her. He gently spread her legs further apart and used his tongue to bring her to the edge of ecstasy. He inwardly patted himself on the back when he slid up from between her thighs to her belly.

He kissed and nibbled at her navel slowly moving toward her breasts. He adored the feel of her breasts in his hands and in his mouth.

When he took her breast into his mouth, she let out a primitive moan. As his mouth pleasured her breasts, his fingers continued their efforts between her legs. Chloe was in emotional overload. She was nearly coming off the sofa. She waited with baited breath for him to get to her mouth. She did not have to wait much longer. His lips touched hers and they began to devour each other's mouth with the intensity of wild animals mating. He released a guttural groan. He suddenly forced himself from her mouth in order to breathe. It was during this brief pause that he quickly stood, removed his jeans, underwear and shirt. Before he dropped the jeans on the floor he removed a condom packet from his back pocket and sheathed himself.

He returned to Chloe and the intensity of their kisses continued. Derrin could not wait any longer. He placed one of her legs on the back of the sofa to allow him to easily enter her. Once he was fully and completely inside of her, he pulled in a breath of air. His movements were swift and hard as he thrust inside of her. He wanted to bring her to a climax but feared that the intense pleasure of each stroke would cause him to crest. Fortunately for him, Chloe was not holding back anything. She moved her hips and met each plunge he made inside of her. Within minutes they were both moaning and panting with pleasure. Chloe reached her maximum pleasure first, the trembling of her thighs and squeezing of her legs caused Derrin to follow suit. He collapsed down on her and kissed her neck.

Shortly thereafter, Chloe adjusted to his weight and moved to allow him to lay behind her on the sofa. The movie was still going. She laughed that neither of them gave the movie the attention it was due. Her laughter made the sofa jiggle causing Derrin to open his eyes.

"What's so funny Bugs Bunny?" He asked in a whisper.

"Nothing. I'm just wondering if this movie ever had a chance tonight. It was probably funny and I needed a laugh tonight." Chloe chimed in before she realized she said too much.

"Is something going on? Why do you need a laugh?" Derrin

perked up and propped his head in one hand while he ran his fingers across her stomach with his other hand.

"Well, I was offered a promotion today." Chloe hesitantly began.

"A promotion is good news, right?" Derrin wasn't understanding the problem.

"It would be if it did not call for me to move five counties away nearly to the mountains. I want to have kids one day and I don't think I can make them up in Dahlonega. I don't think there are even that many Blacks up there to begin with. Hmm, it is not for me. No, not for me." Chloe sighed.

"Wow." Derrin paused before continuing. "Bummer. You're going to turn down the promotion?" For a reason not immediately known to Derrin he realized he was holding his breath waiting for her to answer.

"Yes, sir. I already told my boss that I have family commitments but would reconsider in three months. I lied. I am planning on hiring a head hunter next week. Don't get me wrong, I love my job but I am not moving to Dahlonega for three years just to get a pat on the back and a bigger bonus. It's not happening. He will have to find someone else to fill the position. He will be pissed and will want to fire me, so I am going to get a new job before he realizes what happened."

"Uh huh. You have it all mapped out don't you? But things don't always work out the way you want them to. Don't burn any bridges before you get a job offer."

Chloe rolled her eyes. "I am not an idiot Derrin. I will play their game and be the best architect they have. I won't act crazy with them even after I leave. My mama didn't raise no fool."

"Good. Now, let's go upstairs to the bed." Derrin nudged his erection against her butt to send his message.

Chloe slid off the sofa and pulled him up. They both raced to the top of the stairs and entered her bedroom where they remained for the next four hours. Derrin rose to leave shortly before one in the morning. They promised to go on a date by the weekend. Chloe's heart was overjoyed.

CHAPTER TEN

Before Chloe realized it, the work week was over. She completed the task of filling in the design elements for the reminder of the first floor plans. She had not seen Derrin since Wednesday when he came over and polished her toes. She missed his company.

She planned to fix this problem immediately. Derrin had already planned their weekend, beginning with a special trip to the park tonight. For tomorrow, he asked her to go with him to a bowling alley in downtown Atlanta. She was knowledgeable enough to know that the particular bowling alley was a haven for celebrities, street hustlers, athletes and the girls who want a sugar daddy.

She left work slightly early so she would have time to search her closet and debate her outfit and accessories. She was not going to be the laughing stock. She was going to show those girls she could hang with them. If all else failed, she knew there was a hot outfit in Neiman Marcus she needed a reason to buy.

She arrived home in good time since there was no traffic Friday night. She began packing her overnight bag. She started with the simple items first, toiletries, lingerie, jeans, t-shirts, and house shoes. She labored over what to wear to the bowling alley. She narrowed her choices to a mustard shirt that came mid-thigh and a pair of cream snug pants. She doubted she would wear this outfit since the girls at the event would be bold enough to wear the shirt as a dress. She was not that bold or risqué. The other outfit was a yellow wrap shirt with bell sleeves and a pair of skinny jeans. She laughed at the thought that she referred to these as skinny jeans since nothing about them made her look skinny when she wore them. But they did accentuate her butt and she knew Derrin liked rubbing on her butt.

She finished packing and left for Derrin's loft. She arrived around six o'clock. Derrin was listening to music on his iPod while he waited for her to arrive. As soon as she put her bags in the bedroom, he picked up a shopping bag from the kitchen counter and escorted her to his car.

She had no idea which park they were going to visit. She knew there was a summer concert series in a local park and there was a summer movie series at another nearby park. She decided to ask Derrin.

"Are you going to tell me where you are taking me?" She grinned at him and he drove down the crowded street.

"Nope." Derrin did not take his eyes off the road.

"Come on. You know I don't like surprises. Tell me please, pretty please." She pretended to beg him for the information.

"Hold tight we will be there in a few minutes. Relax and enjoy the ride." Derrin glanced at her and cracked a smile. She leaned back in the passenger seat of his Acura and crossed her arms.

She looked around the car. She realized that she never paid much attention to his car when she first rode in it after the Twister night. The interior was black leather. Other than a few cracks in the seats it looked almost new. She doubted it was new though.

"Derrin, what year is this car? You keep it up nicely. Is it close to new?" She was rubbing the seats as she talked.

"New? Not. I wish it were. I have had this car since I graduated from college almost eight years ago." He was happy she thought his car was new.

"Eight years! Wow. You really take care of it. I wish I could say the same for my Lexus. I have only had it for two years and I have rode it in the ground."

"Why did you buy an expensive car only to ride it into the ground?" He frowned his eyebrows and revealed the seriousness of his inquiry.

"It was my dream car. When I finally took the plunge, I decided to go for it and buy what I wanted. I did not take into account my driving habits. Yeah, I wish I had a curb finder on it so my tires don't eat the concrete all the time, but I make due." Chloe was slightly giggling at her own remarks.

"You bought your dream car. I wish I could do that, but I cannot seem to force myself to go to the lot and give them the amount of money they want for the car I wish I had." Derrin sounded like he was daydreaming and not really talking to Chloe.

"Okay, what is your dream car, a Bentley or something?" Chloe added.

"No way. I want the BMW 7 series."

"Yeah, those are nice."

Before he could comment further, they pulled into the parking lot of the Piedmont Park. From the view of the parking lot Chloe had no idea they were about to enter a local dog park. Chloe beamed at the thought that they would attend one of the concerts in Piedmont Park. She grabbed her purse from the floorboard and took one last glance at the lipstick in the mirror in the window shade. Derrin opened the passenger side car door and watched with pleasant anticipation as Chloe moved her long legs out of the car one leg at a time. She stepped out of the car and stood in front of him.

Chloe smiled at him. His heart warmed.

When they began walking toward the sidewalk, Chloe spoke. "Derrin which concert are we attending?"

Puzzled, Derrin looked at her. "Concert? What concert?"

"Oh, I thought we were going to a summer concert series here since it is Friday night and the concert begins shortly."

"I see." Derrin paused. He did not want to disappoint Chloe but he had to tell her that they were still going bowling and were just stopping through the dog park to get her over her fear. He rubbed his left hand down his face.

"Chloe we are going bowling, remember. We are at this park because I want to walk with you ..." The sound of various dogs barking, some loud, some high pitched, and some fast was heard. Chloe glanced around and there were doges everywhere. She saw small miniature dogs who were spinning in circles, but it was the larger breeds who were jumping up as high as their masters that her worried. Chloe's reaction to the sound and sight of the dogs is what caused Derrin to stop speaking. He did not want her to run but he was sure she would hate him for this little field trip.

Derrin stopped walking when he realized that Chloe was not moving, well technically she was moving because her hands and arms were trembling and she looked as if she was about to cry.

He had to act fast. *Think, think*, he thought to himself. He turned to face Chloe.

"Chloe don't be afraid. I'm here with you." Derrin moved toward her and gently grabbed her hands. "I want you to take one step at a time. I got you. I won't let any of these dogs bother you. You need to trust me. I want to help you get over your fear of dogs." Derrin began slowly walking backwards with each step he took Chloe gradually allowed herself to move with him. Her hands were shaking and her steps were timid. After about ten steps she found her voice. Shaky and cracking, the sounds came from her mouth did not seem like they belonged to her.

"Derrin, I don't know about this. There are too many of them. I want to leave. I can't take the thought of being mauled by dogs in the park." Her eyes were watering. She begged to leave. Derrin turned and glanced behind his shoulders. The dogs were unleashed and running all over the place. What Derrin knew and Chloe didn't was that the dogs who were brought to the dog park usually were not aggressive and were actually people friendly. At least he hoped.

Before long Chloe and Derrin were standing in the middle of the play area. A few dogs walked over and sniffed their feet and legs.

But for the most part none of them cared to harm her. Chloe did not notice she eyed each one as if they were bugs crawling around her toes. She cringed and silently cursed Derrin. She concluded that the quickest way out was to let Derrin think she was suddenly cured of her fear of dogs. She released a loud, long breath before she began her acting job.

She released his hands and smoothed her hand over her hips. She forced a smile and then looked at Derrin. *Lord, help me to do this so I can leave.* She thought before she stooped down to pet a brown boxer who was sitting by her legs panting.

She began talking to the dog as if he were a child. "Hi, there, little doggie. How are you today? Are you having fun running around playing with your friends?" With each question the dog barked softly. Derrin bent over and held his palm flat above the dog's head. The dog sniffed his hand and then licked it. He wagged his tail. Derrin nodded and encouraged Chloe to try it.

Chloe rubbed her hands together and then she followed Derrin's efforts. The dog repeated the same action. Before Chloe could retrieve her hand, another dog appeared and repeated the same sniff, lick action of the first dog.

Chloe was worried that her plan was going to fail. Then out of the blue a dog biscuit fell on the ground in front of her feet. She jumped from the sudden movement. Naturally, she reached down and picked up the biscuit. Mistake. In less time than it would have taken her to say her name, the dogs began barking and jumping around. Chloe stood up without dropping the biscuit of course. She backed up from the frenzy and then her natural reaction kicked in.

She turned and took off running back toward the car with three dogs following suit. Derrin took off behind her yelling for her to drop the biscuit and stop running. It was no good, all he could do was press the key fob to unlock the car doors.

Chloe saw the flash of the lights and immediately knew the doors would open when she pulled the handle. Once securely back in the car, she locked the door.

Derrin paused from chasing behind Chloe and the pack of dogs playfully running after her because he could not stop laughing. He knew Chloe was going to kill him, but it was a sight to see her running for dear life from dogs who thought she was playing with them.

Derrin reached the car and unlocked the door. But when he reached for the door, Chloe had locked it again. They played this game of lock and unlock the door for nearly three minutes. He stopped unlocking the door finally and walked to her side of the car. He tapped on the window. He was trying to hide his grin. He tapped again and Chloe slowly lowered the window glass just enough for him to hear her tell him to go to hell.

Fighting a grin, Derrin bent close to the window and whispered, "I am so sorry. I did not know you were afraid of mild mannered playful dogs. I mistakenly thought you were just afraid of the vicious ferocious killer type. Now, that I know I won't put you around cuddly sweet dogs again. I also promise to allow you to torture me tonight until you feel you have exerted the same level of pain on me. What do you say, deal? Derrin was still trying to keep from laughing when Chloe turned to face him. She glared at him with damp cheeks stained from tears. His heart tightened. He lowered his body down to his knees outside the car door. His face was level with hers.

"Chloe, please open the door. I want to make this up to you. Please let me in."

Derrin knew Chloe probably thought he was speaking of letting him in the car, but he was actually asking her to let him in her heart. He wanted to protect her, to love her. He was willing to give it a try if she was willing to allow him.

He continued to plead with her. Finally, he started singing Jodeci's Feenin'. Of course he only knew the words to the chorus and he did not even pretend to know how to sing in tune. But his effort was comical. He screeched the chorus telling her he was feening for her. After nearly two whole minutes of this madness, Chloe began to laugh and she unlocked the doors. Derrin had his eyes closed and was so caught up in his karaoke style rendition of the love song that he was unaware the doors were unlocked. Chloe finally lowered the window, grabbed his face and kissed him.

Derrin was pleasantly surprised. His lips pressed harder and his tongue entered her mouth. He wanted to climb through the window and devour her. When he pulled back from the kiss, he smoothed her hair and wiped the moisture from her cheeks.

"I'm so sorry for causing you any pain. I promise not to do it again." Derrin rose from his kneeling position, walked around the car and got back in the car.

Without thought he turned the engine. He decided the dog park was a bad idea. He glanced over at Chloe when he turned around to back out of the parking space. He caught a glimpse of something in her body movement, although he could not determine what.

"Chloe, we don't have to go bowling. I can call my frat brothers and tell them we will come next time."

Chloe gasped. *He wants me to meet his friends? Wow.*

"Oh, no you are not getting out of the torture that easy. I plan to beat you in bowling and make you kiss my toes in front of all your friends when I win." She joked.

Derrin smirked. "You really think you can beat me in bowling. Surely you can't be serious. You care to make a wager?"

Chloe laughed. "I think I already placed a wager. You just have to accept it. If I win you have to kiss my toes at the bowling alley and if you win you decide. Game?"

"Am I game? You know I don't back down from a challenge. Let me think about what I want when I beat you." Derrin hummed for a few seconds, then he replied. "If I win, I want you to stay over at my place for ten days." Chloe giggled. "That's nothing. I stay over quite a bit now."

"You don't understand. I want you to stay at my home for ten days in a row. No leaving to go home, no separation."

All he could see was her eyelids blinking and battering up and down. She opened her mouth but did not say a word. She briefly looked away from his gaze and stared out the front windshield. A pregnant pause amplified the engine's soft purring sound. Derrin was not moving and Chloe was not talking.

Finally, she spoke. "Okay, you got a bet. But don't say I didn't warn you when you have to kiss my toes in public." The rest of the ride Chloe focused on repairing her makeup to remove the tears and sweat from the dog incident. She had to laugh at the thought of running from dogs who thought she was playing with them. At the time all she knew was that the dogs were chasing her and she needed to run to get away.

Just when she had adjusted her hair and combed all loose strands back in place, they pulled up to the bowling alley. It was a Friday night and the parking lot was packed. There was not a parking space anywhere near the first three rows. They finally found a space and parked. Derrin escorted her to the door with his hand on the small of her back. She loved it when he touched her like this in public. Chloe nearly fainted when she walked in and saw all the women. She mistakenly thought they were just going bowling, but now she saw that the men were bowling and the women were hunting. The women looked as if they were in a night club wearing mini-skirts, short dresses and high heels. There were all types of women present, but after the first fifteen minutes of observing the environment, Chloe realized these women were most likely all single. She frowned.

"Uh Derrin, why does it seem like the women are not here to bowl but to booty shake? I could be wrong... but I doubt it." Chloe turned to face Derrin and he was smiling.

"Your imagination is playing games with you. I admit that not everyone who comes here bowls, but everyone has a good time." Just when he finished his statement he caught a glimpse of his fraternity brothers. He guided Chloe to the booth where they were sitting.

As Chloe and Derrin approached the table, he could hear them laughing about something. Two of his best friends were facing him, but the one talking just stopped. In turn this made the heads of the other two, whose backs were to Derrin and Chloe, turn around. The four pairs of eyes were on them, actually they were on Chloe. Jared, the one who was talking, finally moved his eyes from Chloe to Derrin. He tilted his head as if pondering something.

Derrin walked up and all of them stood for Chloe. He dapped each of them, but he was forced to hug Jared because when he tried to pull his hand away Jared pulled him close. Jared whispered in his ear, "Long time no talk to, we need to talk."

Derrin nodded to acknowledge the comment, then he introduced Chloe to each of his close friends. First he introduced Calvin, one of his good friends from college, then Ennis, his college roommate and aspiring politician, and lastly Jared, his friend since childhood. Of course, it was Calvin who kissed Chloe's hand and told her, "You are sweet as chocolate." Derrin did not get pissed because this was a running joke between him and Calvin. They often did things to aggravate the other when it came to the ladies. However, Derrin was more concerned with Chloe's reaction than his own. He glanced in her direction. Chloe was smiling at Calvin but it was evident that she was on the verge of making a quick retort. Derrin tapped her hand and her words caught in her throat.

Chloe settled down in the booth and began to casually talk to Jared. After thirty minutes of getting to know Derrin's friends and hearing some of his most embarrassing moments, she decided it was time to bowl. Derrin had been standing and talking to people he knew who passed by their booth. Of course, Ennis and Calvin hovered around the area cat calling at the women who passed by.

Chloe rose from her seat and brushed the wrinkles in her top.

Jared also stood. Chloe walked past Derrin with a little sassy move in her hips.

She leaned in close to him and said, "I am going to the restroom, but when I return it will be time to get this show on the road. Let me know now if you want to renege on our bet. Because I like you, and I don't want you to have to kiss my toes in front of your friends." Chloe giggled and began walking off. She turned and added, "Just let me know." She smiled and disappeared down the hall to the restroom.

Derrin hollered back in response, "Not on your life. The bet is on." When he glanced back at his friends, he noticed they were staring at Chloe. He cleared his throat and they faced him.

Calvin and Ennis walked off shaking their heads and laughing. No one knew what brought about the laughter because no words were exchanged. Jared patted Derrin on the back to draw his attention.

"Derrin, what are you thinking? Why did you bring Chloe here tonight?" Jared's expression was serious.

Derrin was puzzled, as he did not have a clue why Jared asked him this question.

"Man, what in the world are you talking about? I brought her on a date. The last time I checked, this is one of the places we – that's you, me, Calvin and Ennis, bring our dates. So the question is why wouldn't I bring Chloe here?"

"You don't see it do you?" Jared pondered. He continued, "She is not like the women we bring here. Derrin look around this place, it's filled with married men who are not here with their wives, gold diggers who are on the hunt and groups of single women and unattached men. The women who come here know the score and play the game, they are willing participants. This is not the type of place to bring a woman like Chloe. She is a keeper and is the polar opposite of the women we normally bring here. She is wife material maybe your future wife."

"Chloe is not going to be my wife, Jared. We are just kicking it."

Derrin tightened his jaw after he spoke. For some reason, his statement made him angry with himself. Derrin was shocked because he had not realized that his friend would be offended that he brought Chloe to their Friday night bowling.

"Well, I like her and in spite of what you say, Chloe is wife material whether you want to admit it or not, Dee."

After a short pause in the conversation, Jared continued.

"You need to be careful or one of the guys in this place will make a move and Chloe will be someone else's wife and you won't have a clue how it happened."

Derrin retorts, "She is not like Nicole."

"I agree, but no one told you to fall in love with a gold digger who left you before she knew you had money."

Before he could respond, Jared patted him on the back again and said, "Don't mess it up. She is good for you. You deserve better after the Nicole debacle. Keep Chloe away from our regular single dude hangouts." He emphasized single dude hangouts by putting his fingers in the air like he was making quotation marks.

Jared walked off when Chloe returned. Chloe could tell that something had just transpired but she did not know what.

Derrin began moving toward her and escorted her to the shoe counter. They retrieved bowling shoes and found a lane.

Nearly an hour later, their game was finally coming to an end. Derrin thought it was going to be just him and Chloe bowling, but instead Calvin and Ennis brought two new lady friends to join them. As the game progressed, Derrin realized that Jared was right. The ladies openly flirted with his friends and him. They did not care he was there with Chloe. Derrin could not concentrate on his skills or on winning the bet with the chatter from these ladies and recollections of Jared's comments. Ultimately, Chloe won the bet. Jared walked up when the game was over.

She cleared her throat and grinned at Derrin.

"I told you I was going to beat you. Now pay up."

Calvin asked, "Dee you lost a bet to the pretty lady? You should have told us you were wagering a bet. I would have helped you out ... for a small fee." Calvin laughed and gave Ennis a high five.

"Derrin the lady won fair and square, so pay up." Ennis egged it all on thinking the wager was for money.

When Chloe sat down she removed her shoes. Derrin lowered himself to the floor and picked up her right foot. She had pretty feet. There was no scaly skin, corns, ingrown nails or marks. The hot pink polish and nail design was actually turning him on.

His eyes caught movement behind Chloe. He noticed his friends were standing behind Chloe. Calvin had his hand over his mouth. Ennis was doubled over laughing. Jared was just grinning and shaking his head. *I won't live this down for a long time.* Derrin thought.

Then without further hesitation Derrin brought Chloe's toes to his mouth. Once he began to kiss her toes he forgot he had an audience. He could not get enough of her toes. He went from kissing them to sucking them. Chloe was giggling when he began but now she was moaning. She tried to pull her foot back but Derrin wouldn't let it go. He loved to make her moan. He decided he would finish at his house, so he stopped and grinned at her.

"Now, that you have won are you ready to go home?" Derrin asked as he devilishly smiled at her. Chloe damn near choked when she heard him refer to them going home. She tried to get her voice back, but could not so she just nodded her head. Derrin went to retrieve their shoes when he heard the other women pondering what Chloe had that could get Derrin to act like he did in public. They wanted Chloe to write a book since they had been trying to get his attention for several months and he barely said two words to them. Derrin smiled and continued to the shoe station.

He returned and they quickly put their shoes on and rose to leave. Jared was drinking a beer. He made eye contact with Derrin before he commented, "Remember what I said. Call me next week." Derrin nodded and they left.

Unknown to Derrin, Nicole was circling the parking lot searching for a parking space. She spotted Derrin and grimaced. She wondered how he could still drive the car he had five years ago. She thought to herself, *Loser.*

When Derrin and Chloe were once again in his Acura, Chloe decided to ask him about the bet.

"Derrin were you trying to let me win?"

"No, why do you think so?"

"It just seems you were not really trying to bowl. You appeared to be distracted. I wondered if you changed your mind and really did not want me to stay over for ten days." Chloe glanced out the passenger side window as her voice trailed off.

"Sweetheart, I definitely wanted to win. In fact, I could not think about anything else other than having you at my house for an extended period of time. But I just could not concentrate with all the babbling going on between Calvin, Ennis and their female friends. It was nerve wrecking."

"Oh. What did you expect? Those women were on the prowl. All they talked about was how much they paid for their clothes, the cars they drove and their nail and hair appointments. Yes, they occasionally inquired about Calvin and Ennis but it seemed they were just trying to determine if your friends had the financial means to support their habits."

"Wow. You heard all of that? I thought it was just me who got annoyed with them."

"No, I wasn't annoyed with them. I am just used to those types of women and how they act around men. Now, getting back to these ten days you wanted if you won."

Derrin's heart skipped a beat but he did not really know why.

"I will agree to stay at your house for ten days straight even though you lost the bet. But..."

"There's a but?"

"Yes, there is. If at any point you think I am crowding your space or getting on your nerves you have to tell me. Deal?"

"Deal!" Derrin was so excited. He drove directly to Chloe's house for her to pack her bags.

After putting three suitcases of clothes, one duffel bag of toiletries and makeup, and two suitcases of shoes in his trunk, he briefly wondered if he was ready for this.

<hr />

Meanwhile, back at the bowling alley Nicole wandered through evaluating the male prospects. She finally ran into Calvin and Ennis laughing. She joined them by the bar.

"What's so funny guys?" She asked.

Calvin and Ennis glanced at her and paused their conversation. Calvin burst out laughing again almost as if he was laughing at her.

Ennis finally spoke, "We were laughing at the video we got of Derrin kissing and sucking his lady friend's toes after he lost a bet."

Calvin added, "It was hilarious. I never would have thought a millionaire would be reduced to such lows over a bet."

Did he say millionaire? Nicole pondered.

"Millionaire, oh the lady was a millionaire?" Nicole figured her reverse psychology would get her the confirmation she was seeking.

"I don't know if Chloe is a millionaire or not but I was referring to Derrin." Calvin said and chuckled a little more.

"Derrin a millionaire, when did that happen?" Nicole tried to keep her excitement at bay, she did not want to cause his friends to stop sharing vital information.

Ennis was glad to respond to this last question. He added, "Dee has been a millionaire for over five years now. I thought you knew since you were engaged to him during that time." Ennis fought to keep his composure when he saw Nicole gasp and place her hand over her throat.

"Derrin was too cheap to be a millionaire when we were together. Plus, he would have told me something like that." Nicole seemed to be talking to herself more than she was to either Calvin or Ennis.

"Well, he's still cheap. What does that have to do with anything? He has a successful company, an internet café and a healthy sex life. He couldn't be happier." Ennis added for good measure.

Even though the two friends thought they were avenging Derrin, in actuality they were sharing too much information with Nicole. She was going to use every piece of information to her advantage.

Nicole thought, *It seems I need to rekindle my relationship and become Mrs. Derrin Reynolds once and for all. Move over missy.*

CHAPTER ELEVEN

For the next month, Derrin and Chloe spent time together like husband and wife. They had created a pattern for each of their days. They did everything together. They cooked, watched television, showered and bathed, folded clothes and cleaned up together. Chloe was in heaven. She occasionally went by her house to check on things and made sure all was well. On the weekends, they continued the same pattern which also included going to the grocery store together and the café.

At dinner on this particular Friday night, Derrin realized his life would never be the same. He had hidden his heart and stayed out of touch with his emotions so much that he was not aware that his heart had escaped his death grip and landed in Chloe's hands.

He sat and watched her eat her meal. She laughed and giggled about a television commercial she thought was funny. He admired her beauty and compassion, but most of all he loved everything about her. He was not going to attempt to determine when or how it happened, all he could do was accept that it had happened. It could have been when she smiled at him, cooked for him, dozed off to sleep beside him, or took care of him the time he slipped in the café. He was not sure of the catalyst for his love nor did he care. He did realize it was too soon in their arrangement to share his confessions of love with Chloe, that was the one thing he did know. Chloe was leery of having her heart broken and she confessed her love for him before they even started their arrangement. He did not want her to assume his love was mistaken for the comfort level they had achieved with each other.

Dinner ended and he cleaned up the dishes. He confessed to himself that he enjoyed catering to her and sharing his space with her. Chloe decided to shampoo her hair in the shower.

Derrin went into the bathroom to retrieve a nail clipper and was breathless as he eyed her wet, smooth caramel skin. Chloe's eyes were closed as she leaned backwards to rinse out the shampoo. Derrin immediately felt an urgent need to join her in the shower. He stripped his clothes off and opened the glass shower door.

"Hello" was all he could say when he entered the shower as he kissed her neck.

"Uh, what are you doing in here?"

"I thought you needed some help. You know me – your ever ready helpmeet." He smiled and removed the retractable shower head. He began to run the water over her head. Once the soap was removed, he changed the spigot pressure to light massage and guided the pulsating water over her body. He stared into her eyes as she watched him. She was speechless not thoughtless.

Did he call himself my helpmeet? I know he has no clue the religious implication of his remark. He basically called himself my husband. She attempted to shake these thoughts from her head. She decided not to inquire as it may interrupt the mood.

Once they finished showering, Chloe exited the shower first. She dried her hair with a towel and applied hair care products. It was then that Derrin realized his bathroom counter had been converted to her personal beauty counter. His items had been relegated to the corner. He did not mind one bit. At this point all he wanted to do was to pleasure the woman he now realized he loved. Within minutes he was completely dry and pulling her to the bed. They basked in each other's touch throughout the night.

The next morning, Chloe vaguely heard voices in her semi-sleep state. She rolled over in the bed and noticed she was alone. She knew Derrin was in the loft because she heard him talking. While, his voice echoed throughout the open air living space, he was not audible enough for her make out anything he was saying. She pulled herself from the bed and decided to take a shower. She did not have any plans for this beautiful Saturday, but that was okay with her. She would read a book and lounge around the loft. Of course she should go and check on her house, pick up her mail and air out her place, but none of those activities were as fulfilling as being with Derrin. They had moved from being simple acquaintances to comfortable lovers. She enjoyed the easy conversation and quiet moments they shared.

She quickly showered and dressed in a t-shirt and workout shorts. As she traveled down the stairs to the kitchen area, she realized that Derrin was no longer talking. She heard utensils clicking against a plate or bowl of some sort. She knew Derrin did not really cook so he likely was trying to rummage for breakfast.

As she entered the kitchen she stopped and watched him. He was standing against the counter bare chest. His chocolate brown muscles were firm and his skin was smooth. Her eyes admired him from his head to the trail of soft hair that made a path from his abs to beneath the waist of the pajama pants he wore. He was standing eating a bowl of cereal. He appeared to be concentrating on each scoop. He was unaware of her presence at least that's what she thought.

"You know it's rude to stare at people." Derrin said half laughing. His brown eyes met hers and her heart melted. She thought *I love this man.*

"I was not staring at people, I was admiring you. There is a difference in the two." She crossed her arms and wondered what his comeback would be.

He smiled without further comment. She walked closer to him and he put down the cereal bowl.

"What are your plans for today?" He finally asked her.

"Absolutely nothing. I might read a book. Why? Do you have plans for us?" Chloe tilted her head to gauge his response.

"Well, I have plans for you. If you are not doing anything, Kenya and my mom are coming by to pick you up in about an hour to go to the outlet mall."

Chloe was stunned and speechless, when she found her voice she said, "Come again." Derrin smirked, but bit his tongue and did not make a sexual remark.

Finally she asked him, "You actually want me to spend the day with your mother? Isn't that more than our deal would allow?"

Derrin shrugged his shoulders. He knew he had fallen in love with her but wanted to see if she could get along with his mother. It was not a deal breaker if she and his mother clashed but he at least needed to know. He wanted his family to love her as much as he did. Even though his mother never said she did not care for Nicole, he knew she despised the ground Nicole walked on. He gathered his thoughts before he responded.

"You spend time with them anyway. This is no different."

"Wrong. When I spend time with your mother it's because Kenya has invited me or I am doing something with your sister. This time you are asking me to spend time with your mother. This is definitely not the same. I will be constantly aware that I am with them because you sent me. I don't want to send the wrong message to either of them." Chloe was rubbing her hands together as if she was really worried about the idea of shopping with her best friend and her lover's mother.

"Chloe, I want you to go shopping. Buy yourself something nice. You deserve it. Don't worry about anything else and certainly don't worry about the impression my mother may have about me sending you with them." Then Derrin pulled open one of the kitchen drawers and retrieved a handful of money. He put the money in Chloe's hand.

"Here is $600 use it as play money. Go have fun and buy yourself something nice." Derrin went back to eating his cereal. Chloe frowned.

"What's wrong? If it's not enough I have more in my wallet." He sincerely inquired.

"Derrin, $6 would have been enough since it is the thought that counts. I am just surprised by all this."

He laughed, kissed her and walked out of the kitchen.

⸻

By the time Kenya rang the doorbell, Chloe was a nervous wreck. She was worried about what Derrin's mother would think of her spending the night over at the loft. She was also concerned about whether Mrs. Reynolds considered her a sufficient companion for her son. Chloe knew there was only one way to find out – go on the shopping spree. Chloe figured by the end of the day she would know one way or the other whether or not his mother liked her, even though it should not have mattered one bit.

Derrin was in the middle of kissing Chloe senseless when Kenya rang the doorbell. Derrin leaned back a little to evaluate Chloe's response. She was biting her lip and avoiding eye contact. He let her hands go and went to the door.

"Hey big head. Hi Mom." Derrin said as he kissed his mother on the cheek.

"Darling how are you?" his mother responded.

As Mrs. Reynolds moved closer inside the loft, Derrin pulled Kenya to the side. He gave her a bear hug and whispered in her ear, "Ken, please make sure Chloe has a good time. I gave her some money but I am putting a little more in your back pocket. I want you to get her a Coach purse. If this is not enough spot me." He began to rub his knuckles across her head to give the impression to his mother and Chloe that he was playing with his sister. It worked neither of them were aware of the conversation.

"Chlo, you look nice. I hoped you are dressed for lots for shopping."

"Yes, I have on spanks and a pushup bra. Plus I can change out of these clothes pretty quickly with ease."

"Whoa, hold up. I thought you were going shopping not to the stripper bar." Derrin exclaimed. Chloe blushed

Kenya simply rolled her eyes. "You idiot. When women shop they like to try on the clothes to see how they feel. So we have to wear undergarments that help us see the finished product."

"Oh. Well you better say something." Derrin teased his sister. He kissed Chloe goodbye and spanked her butt. She blushed again.

The entire shopping spree was fun. They went to each and every store in the outlet mall. Chloe tried on quite a few outfits, but Kenya vetoed each one. She finally informed her that she needed to throw caution to the wind and look at outfits that accentuate her body. After some prodding, Chloe loosened up and found several outfits. It was Derrin's mother who convinced her to try on the sexy lingerie at Victoria's Secrets. They initially went in to get new matching bras and panties that were on sale. If Chloe did not know any better she would have thought his mother was trying to get her buy the provocative wear to please her son. She was taken aback by it but not ashamed.

They finally ate dinner and discussed the latest Hollywood gossip. Chloe enjoyed the time with both of these women. From the conversation and stories about Derrin, his mother quickly concluded Chloe was in love with her son. She hoped and prayed Chloe would be able to melt the iceberg around Derrin's heart so he could experience love. Mrs. Reynolds was well aware that Derrin believed he was in love with Nicole but she watched their interaction for nearly two years. Based on her observations she knew Derrin was infatuated with Nicole but not in love with her. She also knew infatuation was often temporary passion which led to irrational behavior. Her son had mistaken his feelings for Nicole with love. She hoped with Chloe he would see and feel the real love of a mate.

They ended the trip at the Coach store. By then Chloe had spent the $600 from Derrin plus some of her own money.

"Ken, I'm sitting this one out."

"Why? I thought you wanted a new Coach bag?"

"I do but girl I need to save my money. Buying an expensive purse is frivolous." Chloe glanced around the store and saw hundreds of colorful luxury bags.

"Would it matter if it was someone else's money?" Kenya inquired.

"So long as it is not my money I have no reservations."

"Good. Then shop."

"Huh?" Chloe was confused.

"Derrin gave me money to buy you a Coach purse. I don't have a spending limit. So, shop."

Chloe opened her mouth to speak when Mrs. Reynolds cut her off. "He must really care about you. You know he is as cheap as they come." Mrs. Reynolds laughed and walked off. Chloe turned and watched the older lady admire the scarves hanging on a nearby rack. She excitedly picked out several Coach bags.

Chloe arrived back at the loft with more bags than the three of them could carry. She was beaming with joy even though she was exhausted.

Derrin thanked his mother and sister for spending time with Chloe.

"My pleasure, son. You know she's a keeper." His mother then glanced at the cross-stitch portrait and looked over her shoulder at her son. Derrin's eyes followed her gaze. She and Kenya exited the loft without further comment.

CHAPTER TWELVE

It was a bright sunny Tuesday morning. Nicole had surfed the internet and combed the phone books looking for the internet café Derrin owned. She visited a few in the Atlantic Station area, but quickly learned she had not found the right one. Then she noticed there was one location on her list which was in Alpharetta. She decided to skip the others before it on the list and give this one a try.

She arrived in the middle of the morning rush hour. She sat at a table in the back of the café and watched the crowd. Ms. Kaye approached and asked to take her order. Nicole examined the older lady and decided she was not a threat.

"Yes, I will have a chocolate latte with extra whipped cream." Nicole placed her order and returned to her laptop in hopes of giving the impression that she was a regular customer.

When Ms. Kaye returned she placed the drink on the table along with coffee stirrers and napkins. She asked Nicole, "Is there anything else I can get for you?"

Nicole looked up and asked, "Is the owner here today? I would like to speak with him."

Ms. Kaye assuming something was wrong with the customer service inquired as to the reason for requesting to see Derrin.

"Is there something wrong? If so, I can fix it."

"No, ma'am. I just wanted to say hello. I knew him before he opened this café and wanted to catch up with him. Derrin Reynolds owns this place right?"

"Yes, he does, but he is not here yet. He usually comes in before seven in the morning but lately he has been getting in after nine. If you leave your name and number I can give it to him."

"Sure, I would like that." Nicole responded then quickly jotted her name and phone number on a napkin. She handed the note to Ms. Kaye and smirked. Ms. Kaye put the note in her apron and walked back to the kitchen. Once behind the doors of the kitchen, Ms. Kaye read the note, which said *Hi, sweetie. I really need to talk to you. I miss you and I realize that I was wrong. I am ready to be Mrs. Derrin Reynolds. I am even wearing my ring again. Love always, Nicole 555-342-6778.*

Ms. Kaye huffed. There was no way she was going to give Derrin this note. He was happy with Chloe and nothing needed to interfere with his happiness. She then balled the note up and tossed it in the trash can.

Nicole took one last assessment of the café before she left. She concluded that Derrin was one franchise deal from being able to provide the lifestyle she wanted and she needed to focus her efforts on getting back in his head by way of his bed. She sipped the last of her drink, packed up her belongings and left the café to implement her plans.

For the next week, Nicole called the café every day. She was hoping to catch Derrin when he arrived, but she was not fortunate. She even called when she knew the café was closed so she could leave a message. However, after several messages she had not received a phone call from Derrin. Surely, he was not still angry with her for calling off their engagement. She did love him then it was just that she loved herself a little more. She wanted guaranteed financial security and Derrin was barely making ends meet, at least that was what she thought. He could not afford to sponsor the lifestyle she had become accustomed to at the time. So when she met an investment banker she dated him in hopes of marrying and birthing children quickly. But for the prenuptial agreement his mother wanted him to make her sign, she would have been married and divorced by now. She refused to sign the agreement since it did not provide the amount of alimony that she expected. In fact, she would not get any alimony unless she followed a budget for the first five years of their marriage, gave birth to at least two children and maintained employment during the times she was not pregnant. She thought the whole agreement was akin to indentured servitude and refused. He packed up her things and had them shipped to her sister's house then changed his locks and phone numbers.

Now she was sitting in her one bedroom condo plotting her plans to get Derrin back, especially since she learned he was a self made millionaire. She had waited over a week for him to call and there was no luck. She was unaware that Ms. Kaye had discarded her note and would delete her voicemail messages each day before Derrin arrived.

Nicole tapped her pencil on the kitchen table. *I need to get Derrin to call me. If he won't call when I am being nice, then I guess I have to do something to piss him off. He would definitely call if I made him angry. How can I invoke his anger?*

Four hours later Nicole was pulling up at Derrin's parents' house. She decided to wear a conservative sundress as not to ruffle his mother's feathers but to catch his eye if he was there by chance.

Nicole parked her silver Mercedes Benz in the driveway. She walked to the front door as the sounds from her four inch heels echoed in the air. She pressed the doorbell and turned her back to the door. After a few seconds, she heard a man ask who was at the door. She smiled knowing she had a way with men.

"It's Nicole." She said as she turned around to face the door. The clear glass storm door was the only barrier between Nicole and her potential father-in-law. He had a puzzled look on his face.

Derrin's father slowly opened the door. "Hello Nicole. What brings you here?"

Nicole batted her eyes and began her Oscar winning role as the regretful former fiancé who wants to make things right with the man she loves. If she wasn't trying to get in character she would have probably burst into laughter at the thought.

"Hello Mr. Reynolds. I mean Dad, you do still want me to call you Dad don't you?" Nicole seemed to make her eyes tear up on command. Mr. Reynolds stood in the doorway dumbfounded. After a long pause, his wife walked up behind him wiping her hands on a dishtowel. "Who's at the door, dear?" She asked. When she saw her husband standing in the doorway frozen she glanced at the woman standing on the porch. *Nicole.*

"Hi Mrs. Reynolds. It seems that your husband is overwhelmed by my presence. I would like to talk to you if you don't mind. May I come in?" Before Mrs. Reynolds could respond, Nicole had opened the door, stepped in the house and began hugging both of Derrin's parents. To any stranger passing by it would seem like a family reunion of some sort. However, the devil lies in the details.

Nicole sashayed past them and walked to the dining room. She placed her purse in one of the wing back chairs and sat down. Mr. Reynolds studied her every movement, but did not say anything. He was not going to risk becoming the target of his son's or wife's anger by saying one word. He decided to become a statute and watch the whole scene unfold. His wife on the other hand was fluttering around like a butterfly. Knowing his wife was a true Southerner, Mr. Reynolds figured she would offer Nicole something to drink or eat before she gave Nicole a piece of her mind. He was right.

After everyone had glasses of lemonade and cookies in front of them, Derrin's parents began to stare at Nicole. Nicole knew it was her time to shine. She swallowed hard and began speaking.

"First let me apologize to both of you. I did not handle the initial breakup between me and Derrin well. I was heartbroken and did not want to talk to anyone that would side with him. I knew I loved Derrin with all my heart and that I needed to leave him for a while to allow him to chase his dreams before I made him focus on being a husband and a father." Nicole paused for effect. She noticed that Mr. Reynolds was looking through her but his wife was tapping her nails on the glass and giving her a fake smile.

Nicole continued. "Derrin and I decided that we would take a break and when he was ready we would reunite and become husband and wife. He promised to never give his heart to anyone else. In fact, he told me to keep my engagement ring and wear it when I was ready to be his wife." She glanced down at her hand and smiled. "As you can see I am wearing my engagement ring." She allowed a single tear to roll down her face. "I love him with all my heart. These last five years have been hell. I couldn't eat or sleep. I even started talking a psychologist. It was in one of my discussions that she finally told me it was time to rekindle my relationship or die trying." She looked up just as Derrin's mother was rolling her eyes. Nicole knew she had said enough to get his mother to call him.

"I have been trying to get Derrin to call me back but I am running into a dead end. I am experiencing anxiety waiting for him to call me. I even had to call my psychologist to help me deal with the wait. She suggested I reach out to you first for forgiveness and then for assistance. If you recall my interaction with Derrin, you know I loved him and he loved me. His friends have even talked to me in order to help me work things out."

Mrs. Reynolds cleared her throat. "Nicole, I am glad you are getting therapy. I know matters of the heart can take an emotional toll on a person. However, I am afraid that Derrin has not mentioned you in five years and he never said anything about this arrangement you are referring to." His mother paused as if in deep contemplation. "But I guess if he did not get his ring back then you and he must have had some sort of agreement." Mrs. Reynolds paused and looked away. She finally continued, "Derrin is a grown man and we do not control his life. So I cannot make him call you. But I will give him the message."

Nicole jumped up from her seat. "Oh thank you Mrs. Reynolds! Thank you so much! All you need to tell him is that I am wearing his ring again and he will know that I am ready to become his wife." Nicole grabbed her purse and clutched it under her arm. She smiled at them and turned around. Nicole smirked and turned to Mrs. Reynolds. "Thank you for passing my message along to Derrin. See you later."

She then left the house as quickly as she had entered. Nicole stepped out onto the porch and placed her sunglasses back on her face. She knew she had achieved several goals with this little appearance. First, she knew Derrin would call if for nothing more than to curse her out. Second, she knew Kenya would find out about her visit and be upset, which was yet another reason for Derrin to call her. Feeling great about the prospects, she stepped off the porch and headed for her car. She did not notice there was another vehicle in the driveway until she heard the door open.

She immediately noticed a woman with a nice figure, which Nicole assumed the woman was trying to downplay with conservative yet sexy business attire. The woman's curly brown hair was flowing in the wind and she seemed to be very professional and classy. Nicole hated her immediately. Then it dawned on her that this was either one of Kenya's friends or the woman Derrin's friends were talking about at the bowling alley. *I wonder if this is the person who got Derrin to suck her toes in public. Hmm.*

Nicole slowed her steps to prolong her exit. When she was within two steps of Chloe, she stretched out her hand. "Hello, I am Nicole. Are you a family friend?"

"Well, yes you can say I am a family friend. I'm Chloe." She was startled by the abruptness of Nicole's introduction.

"Nice to meet you Chloe. I did not mean to scare you, but I'm trying to get reacquainted with Derrin's family and friends. It has been hard since we have not been in touch for such a long time. But you know how love goes. It's like riding a bike, you just pick up where you left off." Nicole smirked and squinted up her nose.

"Nicole? Are you Derrin's ex-fiancé?" Chloe attempted to sound nonchalant but she was trembling inside.

"Yes, I am Nicole. But you know when you are the first love you can never be an "ex" anything." Then Nicole wiggled her ring finger to direct Chloe's attention to the engagement ring.

Chloe smiled and walked past Nicole to the front door. Chloe was so upset she forgot to ring the doorbell or knock. Instead, she just opened the door and walked in. The shocked look on Derrin's mother's face told the story. His father just bowed his head and huffed. Chloe had to save her dignity.

"Hello Mr. and Mrs. Reynolds. How are you today?" Without waiting for a response Chloe lifted up the bag she was bringing to Kenya and looked around for a place to put it.

Mrs. Reynolds was standing close to the door and noticed that Nicole was just getting in her car so she assumed the two women had a discussion in the front yard.

"Chloe we are fine. How are you?" Mr. Reynolds looked up and made eye contact with his wife. Chloe just watched the silent conversation play out in front of her.

"I'm fine. I just came by to drop off this bag for Kenya. I will put it here and be on my way." Chloe felt like running home. She turned toward the door to leave, when Mrs. Reynolds softly touched her arm.

"I don't know what is going on, but you need to talk to Derrin. I am sure things are not as they seem."

With a shaky voice Chloe replied, "There is nothing to talk about Mrs. Reynolds. Derrin and I have an understanding and anytime he wants to end things he can. He has not said anything yet, so I am trusting that he is not planning to see any other woman including his ex." Chloe fought the tears, turned on her heels and left.

Derrin's mother sat down at the dining room table with her husband to discuss everything that had transpired. They both decided not to tell Derrin about Nicole's visit because neither of them believed Derrin had rekindled his relationship with Nicole. However, his mother could not get over the fact that he allowed Nicole to keep the engagement ring. She wanted a reason for his inability to retrieve the ring, but she knew the answers would come soon enough. Mr. Reynolds was happy no one was angry with him.

CHAPTER THIRTEEN

D errin finally decided it was time to make things official between him and Chloe. He acknowledged that they had not been together for a long time, but he felt as if he had known her all his life. He believed in his heart that she was his wife. She was caring, independent, resourceful, fun and sexy. He could not expect anything more from the woman he loved. He did not want to accept the fact that he was in love with Chloe, but as each day passed he could no longer deny it.

He knew it would take her a while to accept his pledge of love to her, but he wanted to claim her as his woman. Chloe's birthday was coming up and he wanted to buy her something to symbolize their future. *An engagement ring would be perfect*, he thought.

The last time he purchased an engagement ring for a woman, he did so on his own. He was overwhelmed by the selection process and the anxiety he felt when he thought that he did not pick the right one. This time he was going to get his sister to assist him. Kenya loved Chloe and had begun to drop hints that she felt Chloe was his soul mate. Of course, Derrin never said a word. He allowed Kenya to think she was working on convincing him of this fact, while secretly knowing he was in love with Chloe.

Bright and early on this Saturday morning, Derrin drove to his parents' home to solicit Kenya's help. He did not want to come out and tell Kenya that he wanted to ask Chloe to marry him. He decided to take Kenya to the jewelry store and she would know immediately.

Derrin walked into Kenya's bedroom where she sat in her pajama top and shorts polishing her fingernails.

Derrin began to tease Kenya as usual.

"I would think that a woman of leisure like yourself would go to a spa to get her nails manicured. I'm surprised by your actions every day." Derrin choked back his laugh.

Kenya was blowing her wet nails and did not even look in his direction.

"What do you want? Why are you here? Better yet why are you in my room? I need to call pest control to get you removed."

Derrin grinned, he loved the banter between him and his sister.

"Oh you got jokes. You better stay on your toes because I'm going to get you back for that one." They both laughed.

Derrin continued, "Hey, I need to get Chloe a birthday present and I thought you would want to go with me to pick out something nice for her. You game?"

Kenya jumped up and began fanning her hands.

"I am always game to go shopping." She walked into her closet to find an outfit.

"Well, get dressed and come downstairs so we can go." Derrin turned and walked out the room, but he paused and yelled from the stairs, "Ken, don't take forever finding something to wear. I want to leave before the sun goes down, which only gives you ten hours."

"Funny, you got jokes. Whatever." Kenya selected a sundress and began her transformation. An hour later she glided into the den and announced she was finally ready. "It's about time." Derrin shook his head and exited the house. Kenya could have cared less that Derrin was agitated at the amount of time it took her to get dressed. She strolled to his car like she did not have a worry in the world.

They finally pulled into the parking lot of a local jeweler. Kenya looked up at the storefront.

"You know I thought we were going to the mall. I would never have guessed you would want to purchase jewelry."

"I guess you don't really know me then."

Kenya cocked her head and tried to read him. He was smiling as wide as he could form his mouth. She knew he was trying to get under her skin, but there was something about his behavior that told her this was about more than buying Chloe a birthday present.

They entered the store and the representatives were standing around the counters in black business suits welcoming them in. The store was the typical jewelry store with glass top counters for watches, bracelets, earrings, and rings.

The white male representative approached them. "Welcome to TM Baxter. How may we serve you today?"

Derrin could not say anything before Nicole responded.

She told him, "We are looking for a birthday present for my brother's girlfriend." She grinned at the man.

"We can certainly assist you in selecting something beautiful. What do you have in mind?"

Kenya walked to the first counter and announced, "Something that says I love you but I'm too scared to tell you. Do you have anything like that?"

Derrin shrugged his shoulder and pulled out his cell phone. He decided to remain silent and let Kenya go through her routine. Derrin played a game on his cell phone and waited. After Kenya admired nearly ten tennis bracelets, she finally narrowed the selection to three bracelets.

"Derrin it's time for you to pick. Do you like this one with the princess cut diamonds for $2,000, this one with the diamonds and emeralds interchanged for $5,675 or this one with the larger cut diamonds for $9,900?"

He kept playing a game on the cell phone. He did not display any interest in the bracelets.

"Derrin, I'm talking to you." The salesman watched with his plastered on smile.

Derrin looked at the bracelets and then spoke.

"Enny, menny, minny, moe catch a diamond by the toe, if its dull let it go, enny, menny, minny, moe." His finger landed on the diamond and emerald one. "I'll take this one."

Derrin walked away and headed for the ring counter. Kenya stood in disbelief. *Surely he has gone crazy. My brother, the cheap millionaire, is making financial decisions using a childhood guessing game. No way.*

She scurried behind him.

"Derrin, why did you drag me down to an exclusive jewelry store early on a Saturday morning? Surely, it was not to buy a bracelet that you could care less about. What's going?"

Derrin leaned on one arm and tapped the glass counter next to him. "I'll buy the bracelet, but this is what I came to get."

Kenya glanced down and recognized the rings and bands as the engagement collection. She squealed and jumped up and down. She grabbed him around the neck and kissed him on the cheek.

"Calm down, you're embarrassing me. Geez."

The salesman spent another two hours viewing the various diamonds and settings and discussing carat, metal selection and insurance. Finally, Derrin and Kenya both agreed on the 2 carat pear shaped solitaire with three smaller emerald diamonds on each side.

"Mr. Reynolds we will size the ring and clean it. It will be ready for pick up next week. Will this be sufficient time for the birthday?" The salesman sincerely inquired.

"Next week is fine. I will give her the matching tennis bracelet if the ring is not back yet."

Kenya was beside herself. She knew her friend would love the ring.

CHAPTER FOURTEEN

For Chloe, the next three weeks passed by a little slower than the first two months with Derrin. She tried to pretend she was not hurt by the encounter with Nicole, but she could not get rid of the image of the sparkling diamond on her ring finger. She knew at one point Derrin had given the ring to Nicole to pledge his love and to propose to become her husband. The thought of another woman claiming him as her husband made Chloe sick to her stomach. Even though she dreaded the feelings of inferiority she could not shake how she felt.

While, she hoped Derrin would tell her when he wanted to end their fling. Chloe knew she would have to wean herself from wanting to be with Derrin and be a part of his life. Sadly, she put her plan into action.

Chloe was unaware that her demeanor was noticeably reserved. As she sat on Derrin's sofa eating a bowl of ice cream, Derrin came in from his run.

"Hey baby, what are you watching?" Derrin asked as he placed a light kiss on Chloe's lips.

"Oh, nothing. I am really just flicking through the channels to see if anything catches my eye." She responded without making eye contact.

"Are you sure you are okay? You seem distant. If anything is bothering you please tell me. I don't want any secrets between us."

Chloe looked up from the television and debated her response. She could bring up the Nicole incident but that would lead to an argument she was not really ready to have. Her only other option was to blame her behavior on something else. She decided on the latter.

"It's nothing really. My boss is pressuring me to accept the promotion for the Newvella position."

"I still think you should be happy about getting a promotion. But I can understand your hesitations."

"I don't want to move to Dahlonega or anywhere close to there."

"I see." Derrin paused. "I'm sure you will figure out a plan to deal with this issue. Let me know if you need a sounding board. I'm here for you." Then he slowly exited the room and went to take a shower.

Chloe sulked even more. She could not ignore Derrin's attentiveness nor could she let her heart be broken into a million pieces. She sighed. She could not let him know he was the source of her foul mood. *This is not going to be easy. But Mama always said the way to get over one man is to get under another one. I guess it's time to open my eyes and start looking.*

The remainder of the week passed without further discussion of any problems. Derrin continued to suspect something was wrong but decided to accept the reason Chloe had asserted. He did not want to tell her not to accept the promotion because if she regretted it in the future she might blame him. He also did not want to ask her to marry him right now. He believed she would think his proposal was not sincere as they had only been dating less than three months. What she did not know was that he finally had a heart to heart debate within himself and accepted that he had fallen in love with her after his first trip to her house. Derrin wanted to give Chloe time to accept his love otherwise she may have constant doubts.

Derrin changed his clothes and lay across the bed reading his auto trader and car magazines. He had the articles and photos memorized but he still enjoyed looking at them frequently. Chloe entered the room and watched him flip through the pages. She leaned against the dresser and watched him.

Chloe knew that Derrin had a habit of reading the car magazines.

However, she could not understand how he read the same magazines week after week. She could not comprehend it, but she did recognize the longing look in his eyes when he came across certain models. She could not take it anymore, she had to ask about the magazines.

She cleared her throat to let him know she was in the room.

"Please tell me why you love looking in the same magazines day after day." She smiled slightly.

Derrin turned around and grinned like a kid.

"I just love cars. I use these magazines to fantasize about my dream car. One day I will actually buy it." He turned back to the magazine and flipped the pages until he abruptly stopped and sighed.

Chloe shook her head. "What is your dream car? If you have to look at it with type of desire surely it must be a Bentley or something."

"Here take a look for yourself."

Derrin handed the magazine to Chloe. She glanced down and realized he wanted a BMW. It was nothing special to her. It seemed like an ordinary luxury car, especially one he could probably get a loan to buy." She just laughed.

"What's so funny?" He asked.

"Derrin you act like your dream car is a million dollars. You can get a loan for a BMW from your bank."

Derrin sat up. It dawned on him that Chloe was unaware he was a multi-millionaire. He kept this a secret to see if she would love with him without knowing about his net worth.

He patted the bed as he spoke. "Chloe sit down there is something I need to tell you."

Oh, God. What is he going to say? He can't get the car because he has to pay for his wedding to Nicole. Breathe, breathe. Chloe thought as she complied and sat on the bed.

"There is something I need to tell you. I have been keeping a secret." She put her hand on her throat and held her breath. He put his hand on her thigh.

"I know I have never discussed certain aspects of my life. I want to share them with you now. I don't always go to the café to work. I often have to visit my office to handle business. You see, I own this condominium building, the dry cleaners on the first floor and the café. So I don't need to get a loan to buy my dream car." He frowned and Chloe relaxed.

"Well, why don't you just buy the car?"

Derrin huffed.

"I am a habitual penny pincher. I became a multi-millionaire trying to satisfy Nicole. She thought I could not provide for her. I in turn worked long hours and invested every dime I made. I was not really watching the market and was unaware my broker had made some risky purchases. When he told me that he was being laid off, I transferred all my accounts. It was when I went to my new broker that I learned I was worth several million dollars. I was flabbergasted. For the first year I was scared to spend any of it because I assumed my old broker did something illegal to cause the rapid increase. I ordered an audit and learned every penny was earned legitimately. That's when I purchased the building and converted it to a condominium. I quit my job and opened the café."

"Derrin that is wonderful. After your sacrifices, I would have thought Nicole would have stayed and the two of you would have lived happily ever after."

"She never knew about the money." Derrin rubbed his hand down his face before he continued. "I waited until I got the all clear from the audit. The night I planned to tell her, I caught her at dinner with another man. She told me she was going to marry him and she hoped I understood her reasons. She needed financial security and my $65,000 a year job could not provide her what she needed. She went out the door with her new man and I went to the bar to drown my pain."

Chloe took a deep breath and decided to ask a pressing question.

"Did you ever get your engagement ring back from her?"

Derrin stood up from the bed and walked to the dresser. He fumbled with the drawers and turned his back to Chloe. He did not respond immediately. "No, Chloe I did not get my ring back. I asked her to keep it."

Chloe did not want to continue this line of discussion. She assumed from his behavior that he was hiding something, most likely the fact that he hoped Nicole would return to be his wife. *He got his wish.*

Chloe changed the subject back to the car.

"Derrin let's go car shopping. I want to help you make your dreams come true." Chloe pounced up and pretended to be happy.

Derrin pulled a shirt out of the dresser and smiled. He really loved the woman standing in his bedroom.

Derrin drove to two car lots without stopping. Chloe was puzzled by his behavior. Finally Derrin acknowledged that he was searching for the perfect color and he did not see it at either of the lots. They reached the third lot and Derrin actually parked his car. He was smiling like a child on Christmas morning. Derrin walked the lot and admired three different vehicles. He test drove two and narrowed his selection to the black 750 with tan leather interior. He figured he had to get the upgrade package since he was finally buying the car. He told the salesman to complete the paperwork for his purchase.

"Great, Mr. Reynolds. All we need to do is get you in the finance office to handle the loan and you will be on your way."

"Yeah, alright." Derrin had no intention of getting a loan but it was not the salesman's concern.

The three of them walked inside the finance manager's office. After the introductions, Chloe decided to let Derrin handle his financial affairs in private. She and the salesman returned to the sales floor.

Derrin was so excited about the car that he did not initially notice the salesman was flirting with Chloe, but as he sat in the office and watched them through the glass wall, bells started ringing in his head.

From his view, Derrin could see the guy smiling and leaning against one of the cars. Chloe's back was to the glass wall, so he could not see her reaction. Then suddenly she laughed and placed her hand on the salesman's chest. Her hand lingered on the chest for several minutes. Derrin began to get anxious. He sat on the edge of the chair. Derrin became impatient and called his personal banker.

"Barry, I am buying a BMW. I am going to give the phone to the finance manager at the car dealership. Get the wire instructions and send him the $90,000 and whatever else he needs. I'll call you tomorrow." Derrin jumped up and handed the phone to the finance manager.

Derrin yanked the door open and walked up behind Chloe. He wrapped his arms around her waist.

"What's so funny? I need a laugh too." Derrin nearly growled at the guy. He was itching to punch the guy in the face.

Chloe responded. "Oh, nothing. Michael was just telling me about a sale gone wrong. It was kind of funny."

"Is that right? Michael you must be a regular comedian." Derrin snarled.

As he spoke, Derrin grabbed Chloe closer to him. He was pissed and pulled Chloe outside. Chloe was startled by his abrupt change in demeanor. When they reached the lot, Derrin faced her and planted a hard kiss on her lips while he watched the salesman the entire time. Chloe placed both hands on the side of his face to draw his attention to her.

"What was that for?"

"No reason. I just wanted to thank you for pushing me to buy my dream car."

"No problem. It's what I am supposed to do as your friend."

Friend? Is she serious? Derrin stared at Chloe as if she were a stranger. *So I'm a friend now. She was flirting back there with that guy. I can't believe it, she is just like Nicole a flirting cheater.*

Derrin and Chloe finally left the lot in his brand new black BMW

750. Chloe rubbed the leather seats and intentionally inhaled the new car smell. Derrin was quiet. It was obvious to both of them that something changed in their relationship at the car dealership, but neither wanted to dwell on it.

"Uh, Derrin, I need to go to my house to check on the place and straighten up. Can you drop me off? I don't want you to have to wait on me."

"How will you get to work with your car at my loft?"

"Actually I am taking a personal day tomorrow. So I won't really need my car. I will call you and figure out a plan. It's no big deal." Chloe forced a grin as she spoke.

Derrin was getting more pissed by the minute. He squeezed the steering wheel. He was angry but did not want to yell at Chloe, which meant he decided not to say anything.

He dropped Chloe off at her house, walked her to the door and was going inside when she stopped moving.

"Derrin you don't need to stay. I'll be fine. I promise to call you tomorrow." Chloe walked into her home and gently closed the door as Derrin stood alone on the porch.

CHAPTER FIFTEEN

Derrin went to his parents' house to show them his new car. He mustered as much excitement as he could when he drove them around the neighborhood. He loved his parents and as he watched their interaction he longed for what they shared.

Kenya, who was not home when he visited their parents, called him shortly after she heard the news. She asked a thousand questions about the car. She was genuinely happy for her brother for finally doing something for himself. He deserved to be happy.

"Derrin, when are you going to pop the question?"

"What question?" Derrin knew full well what his sister was asking him, but he was not in the mood to deal with Kenya. He was still upset Chloe was flirting with the salesman at the dealership.

"Don't play me. What's wrong between you and Chloe?" Kenya demanded.

"Nothing really. I just found out who she really is. If I was going to marry a flirt then I could have stayed with Nicole."

"A flirt? What the hell are you talking about?"

Before Kenya could finish her question, Derrin had disconnected the call. She was listening to a dial tone. Kenya redialed Derrin's phone number several times, each time his voicemail picked up. Kenya finally left a message for him to call her.

She then called Chloe but the phone went straight to voicemail. She left a message.

Chloe finally called her back the next day. Chloe told Kenya she would tell her about it if she gave her a ride to Derrin's to get her car. Kenya agreed to the request.

When Kenya arrived at Chloe's house, Chloe grabbed her in a bear hug and wouldn't let her go. Chloe was trembling. Other than this sudden emotional display, Chloe did not say a word about what was wrong between her and Derrin. She did tell Kenya about the promotion she did not want to take and how the new position would take her away from her home, family and friends. Kenya noticed she did not mention the impact the promotion would have on her relationship with her brother.

When they arrived at the loft, Chloe greeted Derrin as if nothing was wrong. She kissed him passionately and plopped down on the sofa. Derrin was shocked Chloe had his sister bring her to his loft. He assumed she would have had the salesman waiting outside for her.

He turned to Kenya who was watching his every move. He silently glanced back and forth between Chloe and Kenya. He finally spoke. "Kenya, it was nice seeing you. Good-bye. Chloe and I need to spend time together."

"Don't you two already spend every waking moment together as it is?"

"Please leave." Derrin barked.

"Nope. I want to see your new ride." Kenya was purposefully taunting Derrin as pay back for hanging up the phone on her.

Hesitantly Derrin grabbed his keys and escorted Kenya to the parking garage. Chloe remained in the loft. She used the time to pack some of her things. She pushed the bags and suitcases under the bed so Derrin would not notice she had started to pack.

Kenya finally left half an hour later. Derrin returned to the loft to find Chloe curled up on the bed asleep. He decided not to wake her. He turned all the lights off and attempted to replace her blue jeans with a nightshirt. He searched the drawer and closet but could not find her nightshirt or hardly any of her clothes.

He pondered this new development. All thoughts of concern passed when he looked at her sleeping peacefully. He decided to get under the covers and hold her. He could not place his finger on what was happening between them and he was not going to worry about it this night. He wanted to position his body next to hers and bask in the wonderful feelings of being with Chloe.

Chloe moved to place her body in a spoon position, where they remained all night. *Both of them finally were able to get a full night's sleep. This would be the beginning of a long period of sleepless nights.*

The next morning Chloe and Derrin dressed for work. She left with plans to move her things out slowly and gradually ease out of his life, since she could not brace herself when he said it was over.

Chloe threw herself into the Newvella project and rarely came over to cook and eat with Derrin. Likewise, Derrin did not make arrangements to see Chloe as much. The couple continued to talk throughout the day and see each other at least a few times a week but after two weeks of the distance, they saw less and less of each other.

In between following Chloe to see if she was entertaining any other men, Derrin started hanging out with his friends Calvin and Ennis again. Derrin was getting back in the party scene.

CHAPTER SIXTEEN

Chloe moped around her house longing to be relaxing with Derrin on his sofa or better yet in his bed. However, this weekend he informed her he had plans with his frat brothers and would call her later. Knowing the writing was on the wall for their relationship, she did not bother to plead with him to share time with her. So here she sat in a recliner randomly flipping the channels on her television.

The ringing of her home telephone startled her out of her thoughts of Derrin. One quick glance at the phone and she knew the caller was Kenya. She lifted the receiver to her ear and immediately heard Kenya's enthusiasm.

"What's up, girl! Put on your party clothes. We are going out on the town." Kenya's excitement touched Chloe. She knew Kenya was trying to lift her spirits.

"Party clothes? You know most of my clothes are still at your brother's house."

"I know we can create a sexy party outfit from pieces in your closet. I'm on my way over. Get up and shower." Kenya's statements were more like commands than anything. Chloe did not have the energy to argue, which meant she simply complied.

As Chloe soaked in the long bath, she concluded *I do need to release the pressure of the job relocation and the demise of my fling with Derrin.*

Kenya arrived shortly after Chloe had finished with her bath. Kenya with lightning speed entered the walk in closet and began pulling various tops, skirts, and pants and tossing them on the bed.

"Now, let's create an outfit." Chloe sat on the bed and smiled. She admired her friend's gutsiness.

Based on Kenya's leopard print leggings and matching chiffon top covering a black bandeau bra style top, Chloe quickly assumed Kenya was on the hunt for something or someone. Kenya exuded sexual prowess.

"Ken, what look are we going for tonight?"

"What do you mean?"

"Well, I can see from your outfit you want to be someone's prey, but I am not that bold. Plus, I can't go out dressed too sexy."

"Why can't you be too sexy?" Kenya raised an eyebrow.

"Your brother would die if he saw me showing that much skin."

"Girl, bump him. He is out with his boys celebrating Marcus' birthday. They will probably be at some tittie bar and nowhere near where we will be." Chloe let out a hearty laugh as Kenya began piecing together an outfit. After thirty minutes of Kenya's homemade tailoring, Chloe had an outfit. It was a satin white shirt with navy blue swirls, wide sleeves and a scoop neckline. Kenya tossed aside the satin belt and pants Chloe usually wore with the shirt. The hem barely covered her thigh. Kenya told her that the outfit would be best worn without a bra. Bells began to ring in Chloe's mind when she recalled Cara's advice the night she first slept with Derrin. Cara had encouraged her to go without panties. She left the party crying. Chloe ignored the anxiety bubbling in her belly.

Derrin, Jared, Calvin, Ennis and Marcus were celebrating Marcus' birthday. Initially the group went to a strip club, but Marcus claimed to have seen his sergeant and informed everyone he did not want to be seen by a superior in a compromising position. Even though, he was well aware the real reason he wanted to leave was related to his attraction to Kenya. He could not bear to get himself worked into a sexual frenzy without knowing he could get relief. Kenya was the woman he craved and no other would satisfy him. After their argument three weeks ago, he knew Kenya would not talk to him let alone make love to him. He tried to reason with her that telling Derrin was not wise, but she was not buying it. Marcus told Kenya he happened to like the location of his nose, eyes and lips and telling Derrin about their relationship could cause his face to be rearranged. Kenya marched out of his bedroom and never came back.

As a result, here he was celebrating his birthday with his friends sans Kenya. Sadly, he convinced everyone to come to go to this new club he heard was on the outskirts of the city of Atlanta. The nightclub was filled to the brim with sexy, attractive women.

"Marcus, good idea on coming here. This is the place to be tonight!" Calvin exclaimed as he patted Ennis on the back and entered the club. They immediately went to the back of the club and gained entranced into the VIP section.

Jared, Derrin and Marcus floated around the room checking out the scene. Jared disappeared when he spotted a former lover. Derrin and Marcus made their way to the bar. Both men longed for the women who claimed their hearts but gave the impression that they were enjoying the night.

Derrin and Marcus slowly sipped their drinks, watched the women gyrate on the dance floor, and glimpsed the baseball scores on the numerous television screens in the club.

Derrin nearly choked when he made eye contact with Nicole, the woman to played him for a fool and bruised his heart.

"Watch out here comes trouble." Marcus warned Derrin.

Nicole sauntered directly toward Derrin and stopped in front of him. She was so close to him that her erect nipples grazed his chest. Derrin nonchalantly looked down at her for what seemed like half a second. He looked away and kept talking to Marcus, who was staring at Nicole like she was an appetizer.

Nicole smirked and placed her hands on the bar on around each side of Derrin while leaning closer into his body.

"Hello stranger. I was beginning to wonder if you were still alive."

"What are you talking about?" Derrin barked.

"I have been calling you, sending messages to you through others and have yet to get a response."

"What did you want, Nicole?" Derrin sighed.

"You. Derrin I want you."

Derrin burst out into a hard laugh. He turned to Marcus and elbowed him.   "Man, she is tripping. Did she really say she wants me? Gimme a break. When she had me she tossed me to the wind. Do you believe anything has changed? I don't."

Marcus grinned, then responded, "Who cares, man. She wants you now in a few minutes she might want me or the guy over there, or someone on the dance floor." Marcus said as he pointed to various people in the club.

Nicole huffed and rolled her eyes at Marcus. She expected hostility from Derrin but Marcus could have kept his comment to himself. *He is a police officer for Pete's sake. A simple low income control freak.* She kept her thoughts to herself, but responded to the comment.

"Marcus I am not even going to respond to your broke ass. Even if you had enough money to pay my bills, I still wouldn't give you the time of day." She eyed him up and down making a point to direct her head to his private parts. "There's simply not enough of you to satisfy a woman like me."

Marcus narrowed his eyes. "Nicole, it would take two men to satisfy you, since you are all stretched out of place. You need to give that cat a vacation to recover and shrink back to normal size."

Derrin tried to refrain from laughing, but he could not control himself. Nicole was spitting mad. Derrin decided to intervene to keep her from scratching Marcus' eyes out. He slightly grabbed her hands and turned her to face him.

"Nicole we are done. I'm sorry you think you want me but we both know you don't. Get a grip and move along to the next man." Derrin paused and tilted his head. "Aren't you married to that investment banker anyway?"

"He was not right for me. He was a mama's boy. So I kept it moving. But the whole time you and I have been apart, I have not stopped thinking about you." She rose up on her tiptoes and whispered in his ear, "I especially think about you when I pleasure myself. Now, you can pleasure me. You know it will be well worth the wait, don't you agree?"

Derrin was unimpressed by Nicole's efforts to seduce him. He realized he was no longer angry with her for cheating and leaving him. He actually felt sorry for her. He believed she would rather exert desperate efforts to maintain a certain lifestyle, instead of providing for herself.

In spite of her tugging on his shirt collar and trying to sound as sultry as possible, it was her question that brought him out of his thoughts.

"Derrin, you know we were good together in and out of the bedroom. Don't you want me?" Nicole asked as she gently gripped his private parts.

"No, I don't want you, Nicole. I have not wanted you since the day you brushed me off to go marry the investment banker." Derrin pushed her away from his body. "I have a woman and she is the only person I want or will ever want."

"You must not want her too much because your body is responding to my touch." She bowed her head down to focus his attention on the spot where her hands were. "What do you say we leave here and go somewhere private."

"I'll pass." Derrin responded nonchalantly.

"Are you serious? I heard through the grapevine that you longed for me and sulked for years, now that I am back you want to ignore me.

This is some bull." She paused. "Well, the least you could do is buy me a drink." She realized Derrin was not going to budge.

He waved at the bartender and instructed him to give her whatever she wanted. After he handed the bartender a twenty dollar bill, he slid away from Nicole without looking back. Nicole gulped down two drinks within minutes. *I guess I have to drown my sorrow. Bump him. There are plenty of eligible men in here. I just have to find one.* Nicole proceeded to put her plan in motion.

Derrin and Marcus watched her as she let every willing man in the club buy her a drink. They also watched as she repaid the effort with dances which included gyrating and rubbing all over each and every last one of them.

"Hey man, did she flirt like that when she was with me?" Derrin inquired.

Marcus did not stop sipping his drink. "Of course. She flirted when she thought you weren't looking. How do you think she met that investment banker? She was a gold digger, Dee."

"Why didn't you guys tell me?"

"You were a grown ass man who thought he was in love. There was no way we were going to say a word about the love of your life. Plus we thought you would snap out of it before any damage was done, but by the time we learned Nicole was cheating it was too late you were over."

"She was not the love of my life. In fact, she wasn't even the lust of my life. I realized I did not love her after it was over."

"Whatever you say. All I know is you were not going to punch me in the face for talking about her back then. If it wasn't for Chloe I wouldn't be talking about her now."

As they were talking, Nicole suddenly reappeared. This time she appeared unsteady on her feet. Initially Derrin assumed it was because of her stiletto heels. But once she leaned against the bar counter and started talking he knew she was drunk.

"Derrin you sure you won't reconsider? I promise to make it worth your while." She slurred each word. It was the sound of her car keys that drew Derrin's attention.

"Nicole, go home you are drunk."

"I'm horny too so what are you going to do about it."

"Not a damn thing." He looked over at Marcus and asked if he would drive Nicole home because she was drunk. He quickly declined and advised him to do the same.

Derrin heard his mother's voice in his mind telling him *Son, you cannot let her drive drunk. Think of the lives she may endanger.*

He begrudgingly glanced back over at Nicole, grabbed her car keys from her hand and pushed her toward the exit.

"Does this mean you are taking me up on my offer, Derrin?"

"Zip it. I am just making sure you get home safely, that's it."

———◆———

Kenya drove through the parking lot of three different nightclubs. It seemed as if she was searching for something or someone. Chloe did not care so she did not bother to ask. They finally arrived at a club off the beaten path. By the look at the parking lot the place was filled wall to wall with people. The line for the entrance was wrapped around the side of the building. Kenya and Chloe patiently waited their turn to be granted entrance. As they were standing there, Derrin and a woman come out of the building. He had one hand on the small of her back and had an angry expression on his face. They marched to the parking lot. Derrin opened the door to a car Chloe did not recognize, the woman got in the passenger side and Derrin eased behind the wheel. Chloe watched the scene intently without moving or even breathing. She realized the scene was eerily similar to the one the night of the Twister game, except she was the woman. Chloe wondered if Derrin was extending the same offer he made to her – a no strings attached fling.

As they sped off, Chloe caught a glimpse of the woman and realized it was Nicole, who was grinning at her like a Cheshire cat. Out of spite, Nicole made the peace sign and slightly waved her hand to allow Chloe to see she was still wearing Derrin's engagement ring. Derrin was too focused on driving to notice Chloe or the exchange.

Kenya stood in the line embarrassed and furious at her brother. She did not know what to say to Chloe. Kenya's mouth was still open well after Derrin and Nicole were gone. She turned to Chloe and saw the hurt in her eyes.

"Chlo, I'm so sorry. If you want to leave I perfectly understand."

"Girl, please. We came to have a good time so let's have a good time. It seems pulling women out of parties is Derrin's MO. No worries."

Kenya was cautious and took tentative steps inside the club. " I know my brother. This is not what it seems. He'll be back. And when he returns you need to cuss his butt out."

They entered the club and immediately spotted Jared and Calvin standing by the bar sipping their drinks. Kenya pointedly began her inquisition.

"Why did you all let Derrin leave here with that gold digger, Nicole?" She crossed her arms and huffed.

"What are you talking about Ken? We have not seen Dee or Nicole. But if truth be told, he knows the hazards of dealing with her. We wouldn't need to tell him." Even though Jared was responding to Kenya's question he was looking directly at Chloe. He instantly knew she witnessed Derrin and Nicole somewhere and somehow. He then asked Chloe, "Do you want a drink?"

"Sure. I'll take a Long Island Iced Tea." She attempted to still her voice to prevent him to hearing the hurt she was feeling.

"One Long Island coming up. Ken, you want anything from the bar?" Jared asked.

"No, I'm good for now." She rapidly moved her head around as if looking for someone. She questioned Jared before he left, "Where is Marcus? I thought you all were celebrating his birthday. Certainly you can't have a birthday party without the birthday boy."

"Speak of the devil and he will appear." Calvin said as Ennis and Marcus walked up behind Kenya. All eyes were beamed on Marcus.

"What? Did I walk up on something?"

Jared smiled, "It seems Ken is inquiring about your whereabouts." Jared walked to the bar, while Chloe and Ennis sat down in the booth.

"Is that right? You need me for something, Kenya?" Marcus had stopped directly behind her slightly touching her butt. She turned around to face him with her arms still crossed over her chest. He was giving her his most seductive smile. Kenya swallowed hard and tried to maintain her composure. His eyes grazed over her face, down her chest and landed on her near bare chest. Instantly, his happiness upon seeing her turned to anger, but was not apparent to anyone other than Kenya.

Kenya sucked in a deep breath before she spoke. "I wanted to know if you had any idea why Derrin left here with Nicole." Marcus glanced over at the booth and decided against having this argument with Kenya in front of his friends. He pulled her arm loose and stomped off tugging Kenya behind him. When they reached the room where the pool tables were located, he spun around and faced her.

"I will tell you about Derrin after you tell me why you came out of the house half naked." He was gritting his teeth.

"Half naked? I am not half naked. I have on pants and a shirt. See." Kenya attempted to pull the see through blouse over her bra like top. Marcus glanced down at her breasts and watched them heave up and down. His hot glare watched as her nipples peaked before his eyes. He thought he was going to lose his mind.

"Don't play games with me. You are dressed with your breasts on display and you know it."

"Marcus, you are a party pooper. I thought you liked my breasts, so you should be happy I have them on display." Kenya was intentionally baiting Marcus.

He wiped his hand down his face and leaned back against the wall. "You wore that little top to get under my skin didn't you?"

"What? Please. I was not thinking about you when I got dressed tonight." Kenya said as her eyes darted across the room to stare at a spot on the wall. She would never admit he was right.

"Liar. You wore it to get me riled up. You wanted me to snap in front of your brother so he would suspect something is going on between us." He paused then continued softly, "I want you. I want you so bad I'm aching standing here."

"I guess it seems you have a few revelations to make to Derrin. Otherwise, I will continue to dress however I please."

Marcus sighed. He knew he had no choice but to man up and tell his overprotective friend he had fallen for his baby sister.

"Let's change the subject before I blow a gasket. You asked why Derrin left with Nicole. From what I saw, Nicole was trying her best to get a rise out of him. If you know what I mean." He raised an eyebrow and looked down at her.

Marcus continued, "He told Nicole there was a snowball's chance in hell that he would ever touch her intimately again. She was pissed and decided to drink herself into oblivion. She came back up to him later to say good night and was so drunk she could hardly stand up. Derrin decided he could not let her go drive home. He asked me to give her a ride. But I had a gut feeling you would appear and I did not need any new reason for you to be mad at me. He decided he couldn't let her drive drunk so he took her home."

"You better be glad it was not you I saw in the car with her tonight. All hell would have broken out. Let me give you a little piece of advice, I am not passive like Chloe. I will turn this place out. So if you met any hot tamales here tonight before I arrived you better let them heifers know to keep their distance."

Marcus wrapped his arms around her waist and pulled her closer. He swept his mouth down on hers with a fierce determination. He sucked and licked her mouth until she moaned. He released Kenya whose lips were still pursed.

"Use your key tonight. I will be at the house waiting." He made his statement as he walked off.

The remainder of the night Kenya watched Marcus and Chloe watched the door. Derrin never returned. After her poor attempt to appear to be having fun, Chloe advised Kenya she was ready to go. Kenya swiftly grabbed her purse and exited the club. On the drive to Chloe's house, Kenya recanted what Marcus shared about the interaction between Derrin and Nicole. Chloe nodded and kept smiling, hiding her true emotions as best as possible.

Kenya dropped Chloe off and sped off to Marcus' house. She was driving like a maniac. The pain and hurt she saw in Chloe's expression made her want to choke her brother so she took her anger out on the gas pedal. However, the dampness between her legs and tenderness of her nipples made Marcus her primary target at that moment.

Chloe rushed through her house snatching clothes from drawers and hangers. She packed as much as she could as quickly as her body would allow her. She cried tears of anger and humiliation the entire time.

Kenya parked her car in the driveway of Marcus' house and went inside. Now that she had reached her destination she wanted to talk to Derrin so she could focus on helping celebrate his birthday. She was frantically dialing her brother for the umpteenth time. Marcus was lying in the bed naked as a newborn baby yet Kenya hadn't noticed, as she was pacing the floor. She decided to leave a message, "Dee I thought you told me the ring we bought was going to be for Chloe. So I need you to explain why Chloe and I saw you driving out of the parking lot tonight with Nicole waving her ring finger. From the view I had it looked like she was wearing an engagement ring."

Derrin picked up the phone. "What the hell are you talking about?" He was still angry with Nicole for trying to give him a blow job in the car. The fact he had to call a cab to pick him up coupled with the fact that he could not reach Chloe put him in a foul mood.

"What I'm talking about is your little exit with Nicole. Chloe and I were standing outside when you damn near dragged Nicole to the car and sped off. Chloe was on the verge of crying and you were gone to do who knows what with your little sex toy."

"I did not touch that woman. She was drunk and needed a ride home. Why would Chloe be crying? She has nothing to fear. I love her not Nicole."

"Perhaps you should have told her that before her encounter with Nicole at our parent's home. It seems Nicole told Chloe she can have you back whenever she wants you. All it took was for Nicole to wave her engagement ring to seal the deal. Chloe is trying to appear like she is not bothered but she is hurt. Derrin you hurt her."

"When did Nicole talk to Chloe? Why didn't I know?"

"I have no idea, she did not tell me until tonight when I was dropping her off at home."

"I've been calling her at home but she is not answering. I gotta go. I need to talk to her."

"Silly, she is not going to talk to you tonight or any night. After your antics basically confirmed the impression that you and Nicole were back together, you may have lost her, Dee. I'm sorry."

Marcus cleared his throat and pushed the bed sheets back to reveal his perfectly sculptured body and magnificent hard on. Kenya closed her phone and tossed it on the dresser.

CHAPTER SEVENTEEN

The lunch crowd had departed from the café and Derrin finally got a break. He had been thinking about all the things his sister Kenya had said to him. He could not sleep, he could not focus and he could not find Chloe. He had to deal with Nicole once and for all. Yes, she was wearing a ring he gave her but he gave it to her when he thought he wanted to spend his life with her. He knew he should have dealt with Nicole back when she walked out, but his heart was shattered into a million pieces and he did not want to face reality. The reality was Nicole did not love him and he hoped if she kept the ring she would someday realize he was the best candidate to be her husband. Too bad, it took five years before he realized that back then he loved the idea of being in love. He knew Nicole did not love him but wanted someone who could maintain her lifestyle, but he hoped he would have the time to convince her to give him her heart. *I was such a fool. What was I thinking?*

Derrin decided to call Nicole. After a brief moment of hesitation, he dialed her number and talked to her about meeting to discuss their relationship. He did not tell her that he wanted to have the conversation they should have had five years ago when she ran off with the investment banker, instead he let her believe he wanted to rekindle their relationship. Nicole invited him to come to her house. Derrin pondered the idea. He hesitated in agreeing to go to her house because he did not want to be seen going into her house and have someone run and tell Chloe or Kenya. He also considered other factors, like if he met her in public she would have an audience to make a scene. Again it would get back to Chloe or Kenya. With YouTube, camera phones and text messaging being prominent Derrin did not want to risk any misinformation getting back to Chloe. Finally Derrin decided that meeting Nicole at her house was the lesser of all the evils. He could leave when he wanted to and hopefully control the situation better.

Derrin arrived and parked his car in the rear of the condominium parking lot. He parked close to the retail stores as to give the impression that he was patronizing one of the stores. He wore denim jeans and loafers. It was clearly not attire appropriate for walking through the mud on the side of the condominium building, but he refused to go to the front door. He stepped up to the patio door and after peeking in to confirm it was the right unit, he tapped on the glass sliding door. Nicole came in the room and told him to go to the front door. He shook his head and told her he was fine with using the patio door. She came to the door grinning mischievously. She slid the patio door open and invited him to come inside.

"Come in Derrin." Nicole said as she turned away from him to walk back inside the den. She was wearing shorts that were close to being panties. Her top was ripped across the bottom to show a little of her stomach. He felt nothing at the sight of her near naked body.

"I'm good right here." Derrin declined her offer and leaned back on the railing. If asked he wanted to be able to say he never stepped foot in her house without lying.

"Are you scared, Derrin?"

"Yeah, I'm scared." He let out a forced laugh.

"I won't bite unless you ask me to. I'll be gentle I'm sure that's what you are used to with little miss plain Jane you are in love with."

Derrin chuckled and raised one finger.

"Let me make myself perfectly clear, I am scared but not of you Nicole. I am scared of losing the love of my life. You can try to call her names or make negative comments but it won't get a rise out of me. I know what she is to me and it does not matter what you see or say."

She put her hands on her hips then crossed her arms over her chest.

"Why are you here at my house then? I thought you wanted to talk about our relationship."

"I want to talk about our past relationship because contrary to the lies you are spreading there is no present or future relationship between us." Derrin realized that he needed closure and he wouldn't be able to get Chloe back until he told Nicole what he came to say. But before he could start the conversation, Nicole started speaking.

"So did your girlfriend make you come over? Are you being a good boy and doing what you are told?"

"No, Chloe does not have any idea I am over here. She won't talk to me since you have somehow convinced her that we are getting married."

"Well, aren't we? You let me keep your ring. Doesn't that mean you want to marry me?" Nicole was taunting him, but Derrin was determined to remain calm.

"Hell no, it does not mean that. First, I let you keep the ring because you threatened to call the police and tell them that I was stealing your personal property, then a month later you told me that you lost it when you hid it from your boyfriend. So when you called to tell me you conveniently found the ring I told you to keep it because I did not want the headache. In hindsight, I realize now that I should have forced myself to deal with you once and for all. Maybe then I would not have you interrupting my life now."

"At one point you told me I was your life. Do you really want me to believe you just moved on because you have the eye of some plain Jane? Please. Tell that to someone who will believe it. You and I both know you did not want to get the ring back because you did not want to face the reality that we were not going to get married. You were still hoping things would work out. I talked to your friends and I know you never got over our relationship. So, don't pretend you just didn't want to be bothered. I know you better than that."

"Nicole, I am not going to argue with you or try to convince you of my reasoning. I am here to talk to you in a language you understand."

"What language is that? "

"Money. Cold hard currency." Derrin crossed his legs at the ankles and waited for her response.

"I'm listening. What do you have to say?"

"I will buy the ring back from you. But you have to accept my conditions."

"What are your conditions? I may not want to sell you the ring. Did you ever think about that?"

"Oh, you will sell it. I have no doubt about it. Now, my conditions are simple. First, you have to agree not to contact me, my parents, my sister, my friends, my businesses, Chloe or our children."

"Children? You don't have any children."

"Well, I plan to give Chloe as many children as she wants and I don't want you to suddenly appear causing trouble. Next, you have to agree to post on your Facebook page and twitter that you lied about us being back together."

"If you want me to say I lied then you must have a large number in mind. So, let me hear the figure."

"You give me the number." Derrin was an experienced negotiator and he knew never to bid against himself.

"Wow. You must be in love because your cheap butt would never have said that five years ago." She pressed her manicured nail on the bottom of her chin and hummed. After several seconds she decided to try her luck with Derrin. She was deep in debt and needed to get out before she sank. She encouraged herself. *He has the money and you know what the Bible says 'you have not because you ask not'.* Nicole then grinned and stared into Derrin's eyes.

147

"I will give your ring back and accept your conditions if you pay me $60,000." She held her breath waiting for his response. Nothing was said and no one moved. She continued to stare at him. However, she could not read him. His eyes were expressionless.

Derrin cleared his throat before he spoke.

"Nicole I am not going to pay you $60,000. Now, give me the real number or I will just leave and you get nothing."

"You are still cheap. I thought you loved her, your precious little Chloe. She's not worth $60,000?" Nicole was purposefully baiting Derrin.

"She is worth $60 million but that has nothing to do with the ring you have." Derrin paused then continued, "I will give you $10,000."

"Nope. $40,000." The two of them went back and forth rapidly until Derrin finally said, "$25,000 and that's my final offer. The ring you have did not even cost ten percent of what I am offering. Take it or leave it, it's your decision."

Nicole huffed. "Deal. But I want my money in cash or certified funds. Your cheap butt may place a stop payment on the check before I can make it to the bank."

Derrin shook his head in disgust.

"Fine, you can pick up the certified check from my attorney's office when you sign the agreement."

"Agreement? What agreement?"

"Do you really think I would take your word in this matter? Get real. My attorney will call you. He has your number, you were on his to call list for a prenuptial agreement. You just happened to want to hurt me before he had a chance to call you."

"Derrin, I did not want to hurt you. Whether you believe it or not I did love you. I was just afraid of being poor. I had been there and done that. I was taught a wealthy husband was the only way out of poverty, so I set my sights on finding one. My falling in love with you was an unintended detour." Then without notice, Nicole reached down and pulled the ring off her finger and threw it at Derrin.

"There you have your ring for free. Now, go and marry your plain Jane."

"Nicole..." She cut off his statement when she screamed at him. "Get out!"

Derrin backed away from her and slowly exited the patio. He headed for his car with the ring in his hand. He could not believe Nicole actually gave it to him without a dime. *She is hurting.*

Derrin sat in his car, but before he started the engine he called his attorney. He left him a message to send Nicole a certified check for $25,000. He knew he did not have to give her the money, but he figured she was telling the truth. He realized that in her own way she did love him. It was too bad she did not love him when he thought he loved her.

CHAPTER EIGHTEEN

Derrin called Chloe each day on her cell phone, office phone and home phone. She never answered and she never called him back. Often he simply hung up without leaving any messages.

He sulked around the café day in and day out for nearly a week. Ms. Kaye watched his behavior. She decided it was time to give him her two cents whether he wanted to hear it or not.

"Derrin, you know if you had heeded my advice you wouldn't be in this situation."

"Ms. Kaye what advice?"

"I told you to listen to her. You knew she wanted honesty, so what did you do? Lie to her about your true feelings and avoided discussing your dealings with Nicole. You should have told Chloe how you felt about her." Ms. Kaye wiped her wet hands on her apron and walked to the sink. She continued, "You decided to hold your feelings in and allow her make her own assumptions." Derrin huffed. He thought about the only other women in his life, his mother and Kenya.

"I have to go. I just remembered I need to drop by my parent's house. You have things under control here." As quickly as he spoke he left the café.

Derrin drove to his parent's home. He let himself in and immediately his eyes met Kenya's. She was furious. She stomped up the stairs and slammed her bedroom door.

His mother appeared in the hallway. He wanted to run into her arms but he chose not to revert to his adolescent days. His mother kissed him on the cheek and escorted him into the den. She sat on the sofa.

"Derrin, sweetie. What is going on?"

"What makes you think something is going on?" He tilted his head and asked his mother.

"I am old not blind, even though a blind man could see you are in turmoil and your sister is on the verge of choking you. So sit down and tell me what is going on."

She patted the sofa and he removed his shoes and walked to his mother. He laid his head in her lap and spilled it all. He told his mother what happened at the car lot and the bar.

"So that's why Chloe won't call me back. I don't know what to do."

"Son, you need to deal with Nicole first. Are you aware she came to visit me and your father? She sashayed in here announcing her return and her plans to marry you. She shed her pretend tears and thought she had convinced us that you wanted to marry her. We knew she was lying so that's why we did not bother to tell you. When I saw you and Chloe together I knew you had finally found true love. I did not want you to return to that bad place you were in when Nicole left you. I thought my decision to keep Nicole's visit from you was best."

"Mom, don't blame yourself. If I had told Chloe I loved her then Nicole's visit would not have meant a thing."

"I agree. But truth be told it was the ring Nicole was flaunting that gave credibility to her claims. You need to deal with that issue before you go forward, son."

"I got the ring back." He reached in his jeans pocket and retrieved the diamond solitaire. He raised it so his mother could see it. She smiled and rubbed his cheek. He handed the ring to her and smiled. "You can have it. It has been a curse."

Derrin lay in his mother's lap and contemplated his future. Saddened by the prospects, he went home.

After he arrived home, he poured a glass of Hennessey and coke.

He sat on the sofa in his living room and noticed the portrait hanging on his wall. He finally admitted, *Chloe was right, love can heal all pain.* He raised the glass to his mouth and threw it at the wall. He was angry, lonely, and horny. He missed Chloe and ached to hear to her voice. His loft was a constant reminder of her presence in his life. Her toiletries were on his bathroom counter, her clothes were in his closet, her scent was in his sheets and most importantly her engagement ring was on his dresser. He tried to take a nap, instead he tossed and turned.

Kenya decided to go ahead and press the doorbell to her brother's loft. It was time to get this over with, she thought. She held the two unconstructed boxes in her hand. She anticipated her brother's bad mood.

Derrin opened the door and looked at his sister. He noticed she was avoiding eye contact. It was then that he caught a glimpse of the cardboard she was holding.

"Ken, what's up? Why are you here?"

Kenya pushed past Derrin and walked into the living room. She released a long sigh before she spoke.

"Chloe asked me to come over and retrieve her belongings. She figured two boxes would be enough for the items she was not able to take with her."

Kenya started toward the stairs when Derrin tugged at the tail of her shirt. She stopped on the first step.

"Ken, I love her, not Nicole. I did not rekindle anything with Nicole. I simply gave Nicole a ride home since she was intoxicated. You have to believe me."

"I do believe you and so does Chloe. Chloe claims your relationship was winding down anyway, so it makes sense to end things while things are rocky. She thinks that will make it easier."

Derrin's heart skipped a beat. He needed to see Chloe and show her she was his only true love.

Kenya began to continue up the stairs. Derrin grabbed the boxes from under her arm.

"You are not leaving here with any of her belongings. If Chloe wants her things she has to come and get them."

"Derrin she gave me the key back. She has no plans to return here." Kenya saw the hurt on her brother's face. She felt her muscles tense.

"I need her, Kenya."

"Well, what you need is a plan because I am getting depressed from the misery you guys are in." Kenya handed him the box tops and stalked out the front door.

Chloe waited for Kenya to visit with her belongings. She could not imagine what was delaying Kenya. As she passed the time she reminisced about the good times she shared with Derrin. She could not help the questions that ran through her mind. *When did he stop wanting me?*

Her phone beeped and she realized that someone was calling her. She glanced at the caller id and noticed it was Derrin. She did not pick up the phone. She sat and listened to his baritone sultry voice.

"Chlo please call me. I need to talk to you. I am not going to stop calling you. I want you to know I was not with Nicole. Yeah, you saw me in her car but I was merely driving her home since she was sloppy drunk. Nothing happened. She means nothing to me."

Yeah right. Derrin you have no clue what or who you want. So I will make the decision for you. Chloe continued to hear Nicole's words - *you know when you are the first love you can never be an "ex" anything.*

Chloe decided to call her friend Cara and cousin Diane on a three way call. She told them everything that transpired between her, Derrin and Nicole. She felt a big load lift from her shoulders. She was able to express her true feelings without worrying about being prejudged or discredited. She cherished her friendship with Kenya but because Derrin was her brother, she tended to look at things differently.

Cara was the first to speak. "Chlo, you know me. I can't imagine giving up good sex for no reason. Plus, from the way he watches you, pure lust and love seeps from his every pore. I say give it another try."

"Cara you are a self-professed nymphomaniac so anything involving great sex is a good reason to keep a man." Chloe said causing Diane to laugh.

Diane joined the discussion. "Chloe, I have to admit I agree with Cara. I have had my bad experiences with men, so winning me over is no easy task. I think Derrin loves you. He waits on you hand and foot. I saw him recently and he looked miserable in spite of being surrounded by his frat brothers and women to spare. He has to love you."

Chloe listened attentively to her cousin and friend. For different reasons, the mere fact that they both believed Derrin loved her was amazing.

"Guys it is all a game. Derrin does not love me. He lusts me that's it. And I don't plan to be his sex toy anymore. Cara will you call him and tell him I got his messages, but there is nothing more to discuss. Tell him I hope he has a long happy life."

She decided she needed to make another call.

Chloe pressed the last digit on the phone. When the receptionist at her office answered she took a deep breath. She was transferred to her supervisor.

"Mr. Walker, this is Chloe Dancy. Is the offer still open for the Newella position in Dahlonega?" Chloe stared at the ceiling.

"Of course. The position is open if you want it. Are you sure?"

"Yes, sir I am. Why do you ask?"

"Well, it seems that you were hesitant to accept the offer. I assumed it was because of your relationship and family commitments."

"I am working through my commitments. I think I will have all my loose ends tied within the next two weeks. I want to visit the area and get acquainted with the area before I commit to taking the position."

"Okay. Let me know as soon as you determine this will be an opportunity you want to accept."

Chloe escaped to Dahlonega for next the two weeks. She stayed in a rented cabin and visited all the tourist sites. The area was beautiful. She wished she could have a vacation home here not a permanent residence. As the days went by she cried less and regained her composure.

It's time to return home and face life.

CHAPTER NINETEEN

PRESENT DAY.

Chloe folded her cell phone to end the call. She turned on the ignition in her car and began driving home. She was mindlessly driving along the familiar streets of her neighborhood. She would not really miss the area since she rarely spoke or interacted with her neighbors. She knew her unhappiness was not due to the thought of moving but to the fact that she was no longer going to enjoy Derrin's company.

She reached her street and maneuvered her car toward her driveway. As she approached, she pressed the garage door opener not knowing Derrin was parked in her driveway.

When Derrin saw the garage door go up, he looked up from his magazine toward the street. He threw the papers on the passenger seat and opened his car door.

Chloe realized Derrin was parked in her driveway, she made a sudden judgment call. *Oh shit!* She quickly pressed the garage door opener and sped off down the street. Several rapid turns later she was racing up the main road leading to the highway. Derrin slammed the car door, backed out of the driveway and followed chase. He knew his BMW was practically a race car and could easily catch her SUV, but she had a few minutes jump on him. He was not familiar with the streets in her neighborhood, so he manipulated the subdivision a lot slower than he would have liked. When he made it to the main road, there were no cars blocking his view of Chloe's SUV. He pressed the gas pedal and sped off to catch her. Chloe noticed his black sleek car in her rear view mirror and decided to keep going straight through the yellow light.

Derrin wondered, *Where is she going?* He debated several possible destinations but as she passed prime streets and roads he knew those destinations were not in the plan. He was determined to keep chasing her and not let up until he caught her. Chloe eased onto Interstate 85 North and merged onto Interstate 985 toward Gainesville Georgia, the chicken capitol. Derrin would have enjoyed the scenery but he was too focused on catching Chloe. He was also amazed that his car had not been able to pass her on the open road. He did not realize fear was driving Chloe and caused her to make dangerous maneuvers.

At the speeds they are going Derrin was certain they would be stopped and carted off to jail. He smiled as he thought, *At least we will be together in the patrol car.*

Derrin dialed his friend, Marcus.

"Hey man, I can't talk long I'm in the middle of something. I need your help."

"Sure. Why do I have the feeling this is something I should decline?"

"You know me, man. Hey, I am following Chloe up 985 in your neck of the woods and need you to make sure your cop buddies don't stop me. Well, they can stop her if they want." Derrin chuckled.

"Hmm. I have no idea why the police would stop you if you are leisurely driving up the scenic highway."

"Let's just say we are testing the engines. I need help to get her to stop. Please."

"Okay, but if you cause any accident or incident chasing her up the highway I will disown you in a heartbeat. Be careful man chasing love man ain't easy."

"I'm just trying to talk to her. Any help you can provide is appreciated. Now, I gotta focus on catching my love or it may get out of sight. Bye." Derrin tossed the phone on the passenger seat.

Shortly thereafter, Chloe quickly passed two police cars parked on the side of the highway. She did not even think about pressing the brakes. Within a few minutes Chloe heard the police sirens. In a panic she pulled off the highway and into a small hotel parking lot. She did not attempt to properly park her car, she merely slammed on the brakes, snatched her purse and left the car parked half in one space and half in another. She jumped out of her vehicle and ran inside the hotel.

The clerk was an old white woman who looked as if she did not want to be disturbed. The clerk wore a name tag that read Della on her grass green colored uniform shirt. The lobby was empty and the darkness from the evening light gave the place an eerie feel.

"Excuse me, but do you have a public restroom?"

Della lifted her eyes from her novel and glanced at Chloe. She quickly discounted any threat and pointed to her left.

"It's around the corner. Make sure you turn the lights off when you leave." Della immediately went back to reading her book.

The restroom was the size of a closet and located directly behind the hotel front counter. Chloe swiftly moved past the front counter and into the restroom. She locked the door behind her and slid to the floor clutching her purse.

The squealing of tires interrupted Della's reading. She looked out the glass door and noticed a black BMW speeding through the parking lot. She knew the young man's appearance at the hotel was most likely related to the presence of the young lady.

Della placed her novel on the counter with the pages laying face down. She pondered, *This is going to be interesting.* She crossed her arms over each other and laid them on the counter, while she watched Derrin approaching.

"Good evening, ma'am. I am looking for a young, attractive, black female who was driving the SUV parked out front. Have you seen her?"

Della sucked her teeth.

"Maybe, maybe not. What is her relationship to you?

"She is my girlfriend."

She tapped the sign on the counter which listed the hotel policies. "Sorry we don't give out information to anyone unless they are guests here. And the last time I checked you were not a guest."

Derrin figured Della was trying to be difficult to spice up her evening. He decided to play along.

"Okay. Well do you have any vacancies?"

Della took her time and looked in a ledger. She placed the eyeglasses hanging from her neck by a string on her face and moved her finger over the pages. She cleared her throat and announced, "You are in luck, there is one room left."

"Great. I will take the room, please."

"I haven't told you how much it costs."

"I'm sorry, what is the one night fee?"

"It's $65 plus tax and for a late checkout it is an additional $20."

"I won't need a late checkout."

Derrin removed a $100 bill from his wallet and placed it in her wrinkled hand. She passed the room key to him. Neither of them was aware the local police were entering the lobby. Della turned to give him the change and the officers drew their guns.

"Hold it. Hands up!" Both Derrin and Della raised their hands in shocked response.

"Ms. Della are you okay?"

"Yes, Anthony I am fine. Now put those guns up. This is a hotel not a shooting range." It was apparent Della knew the officers very well. Both officers holstered their pistols and turned to Derrin.

"Sir, why were you speeding through our city like a madman? It's Friday night and high school football is going on. You could have killed someone."

Derrin looked at Ms. Della and she was grinning at him. He

realized she was aware he was chasing Chloe into the hotel and was waiting for his response.

"Officers, I apologize. I was chasing someone who has something that belongs to me." Before the officer could inquire further, Chloe, who heard the commotion from the restroom, appeared from behind the side of the front counter.

Chloe coughed to announce her presence. "I'm sorry officers. But he was trying to catch me. I apologize if we caused any trouble. I was trying to get as far away from my house as possible."

"Well you two have broken several traffic laws, including breaking the speed limit. At one point, I clocked you sir going 92 miles per hour."

"Someone is going to jail tonight."

Chloe swallowed hard. Her hands were trembling.

The ringing sound from the bells on the front door forced everyone to turn around. In walked Marcus.

"What seems to be the problem? Tony. Bill." Marcus asked the officers who wore uniforms identical to his.

"Nothing, we just have a couple of city slickers here who think they can do what they want to do up here in our neck of the woods. We were just telling them they will be checking into our county hotel." Everyone knew the officer who was speaking was referring to jail not an actual hotel.

"Let me talk to you both for a minute." Then Marcus guided his fellow officers to a spot closer to the front door. No one could hear their conversation, but by the random glances over their shoulder at Derrin and Chloe it was obvious they were the subject. The three officers burst out into laughter and shook their heads. Then as abruptly as they came in, Marcus and one of the officers exited out the door. The one named Tony walked over to the three remaining occupants of the lobby.

"It seems there is more pressing action going on at the high school football game and my fellow officers have left to deal with it. And I would like to avoid the paperwork for arresting you two." He paused for impact. "Here's the deal, you either get hotel rooms for the night or you leave the premises. If you don't leave then I will be forced to arrest whoever is left in this lobby five minutes from now." The officer left to go and sit in his patrol car. No one knew there was a wager on whether or not Derrin would fall down in the lobby and beg the young lady to forgive him. Officer Tony bet Marcus breakfast for a week that Derrin wouldn't beg Chloe especially not in front of Della, the other officer figured Derrin would simply leave the headache behind. Of course, Marcus knew his friend would do whatever it took to get Chloe back. He wagered breakfast and a car wax for each patrol car, if Derrin did not totally beg Chloe for her love.

Chloe, spoke in a soft shaky voice, "Ma'am I would like to get a hotel room for tonight."

Della looked at Derrin and back at Chloe.

"I'm sorry but I just booked my last room for the night to this young man."

Chloe swallowed and avoided eye contact with Derrin.

Derrin eased closer to her. When he was close enough to touch her he could see the tears welling in her eyes. He did not want to cause her to cry in the lobby of some hotel.

"Chloe, sweetheart. You can have the room if you really don't want to go home tonight. I just ask that you allow me to walk you to the door."

"Derrin, I don't want to talk you right now. My heart is broken into pieces and talking to you right now will simply make the pain worst."

Derrin thought he would punch something. He never wanted to hurt her, not his woman.

"Here is the key. Have a good night." Derrin hesitantly handed her the key and stood still. Chloe eased the room key from his hand. She stared at it for a few seconds and then looked at the clerk. Who was pointing toward a door.

"The room is down that hallway past the elevator on the left. Cheapo here did not pay for late checkout so you need to leave before 11 a.m."

Chloe nodded acknowledgement and left.

Della tipped her head to Derrin and just watched him. She could see the longing in his eyes.

"So what are you going to do just stand there and watch her leave?" Her voice brought him out of his trance.

"Men. You all are idiots." She said as she looked him directly in the eye.

She shook her head and picked up her novel. Derrin noticed it was a romance novel. He chuckled. *This is probably the most excitement she has witnessed in a long time. Well, I might as well seek her counsel.*

"Ms. uh Della", he read from her badge, "what do you propose I do? You heard her. She does not want to talk." Derrin leaned one arm on the counter.

"Who said anything about talking? Young man, you need to go up to her room and seduce her. You can talk later."

"I don't know the room number. You and I never got that far remember?" He smirked, then continued. "Plus, you don't give information to persons who are not guests."

"Well, since you gave me such a nice tip, I'll make an exception."

"Tip? What tip did I give you?"

"I kept your change from the $100 bill." She grinned.

"I tell you what, if you give me something I can deliver to her room, I will give you an even bigger tip." Derrin knew she would take him up on his offer by the smile that covered her face.

Della tapped the counter and thought, then she exited the counter area. She returned shortly with a tray filled with various chocolates, a vase with a single rose and a glass of champagne. She handed him a waiter's coat and a folded white note card.

"Use your imagination." She informed him.

Derrin eyed the romance novel and smirked. "I could, but I'm sure you would write it better. Oh, by the way, I was telling the truth when I said I was chasing someone who had taken something that belonged to me. The young woman in your hotel room has taken my heart and I don't want it back." He pushed the note card toward her. She became giddy and started writing. Derrin had no idea what was being written on the card, but he knew it would be romantic and effective.

He went into the restroom and changed into the waiter's coat. When he returned, the tray was decorated and covered in a white cloth with the items strategically placed. Derrin opened the card and read it, *This tray is filled with chocolate as sweet as your kisses, with a rose whose petals are as soft as your touch, with champagne as bubbly as your laughter, and covered by a white cloth as pure as your love. This is a special delivery to the woman who has captured my heart.*

Derrin liked the card. He opened his wallet and handed Ms. Della two crisp fifty dollar bills, picked up the tray and put his plan into action.

Shortly afterwards he was standing in front of the door to the room where his love was hiding, probably crying. He nervously wiped his hands on his pants and lightly tapped on the door.

"Who is it?" Chloe asked in a voice which confirmed she had been crying.

"Room service."

Chloe automatically opened the door without looking in the peephole.

She was talking as she opened the door. "I didn't order any room service." She instantly stopped talking when she saw Derrin standing there. He did not say a word. He merely extended the tray toward her.

"Derrin what is this?" She asked.

He did not respond. He just smiled. She grabbed the tray and went inside. She mistakenly assumed he would come in the room behind her. She blindly walked carrying the tray and read the card.

"Oh Derrin!" Chloe turned but the door closed behind her.

She put the tray down and yanked the door open. Derrin had already left and was standing by the elevator. The sound of the door opening made him turn. All he saw as Chloe running toward him. He opened his arms and braced himself for her touch.

He closed his eyes and allowed his senses to overload on her smell, touch, kisses and love. She threw her hands behind his neck and kissed him with all the passion she could muster. Their tongues mated in a sensual dance. Derrin missed this. He missed Chloe. When they finally broke the kiss to breathe, Chloe went to talk and Derrin placed a finger over her mouth. She smiled. Her heart was overflowing.

Chloe pulled Derrin back to her room. Once inside, she locked the door and pushed him against the door. She resumed her kissing assault. She licked around his neck and ears. She sucked his bottom lip and allowed her tongue to explore every crevice in his mouth. Then she proceeded to unbutton the waiter's coat. She pushed the coat back off his shoulders. She allowed her hands to rub his nipples as she licked him while bending on her knees. She swiftly unzipped his pants and pulled them down along with his briefs. His manhood was standing erect. She smiled and raised her eyes to look at Derrin. He simply shrugged his shoulders and grinned.

"I want to apologize this time." Chloe said as she proceeded to take all of him into her mouth. She sucked and licked until Derrin was groaning and growling. She continued until he reached his release. He slumped over and pulled her up from the floor.

"Can I talk now?" He asked her.

"Not really. We have a lot of making up to do."

"You don't say. Well, before we go any further, I need to ask you something."

"What could you possibly need to ask me at this very moment?" Chloe asked giggling as she tightened her arms around his neck.

Derrin bent over and retrieved the diamond and emerald engagement ring from his pants pocket. He lowered himself onto his knees, holding the ring upwards, he asked, "Chloe Dancy you are the woman who has healed my heart. Will you marry me and become Mrs. Derrin Reynolds?"

Chloe was shaking and trembling. She answered through the tears and sobs, "Yes! Derrin, yes, I will become your wife."

EPILOGUE

Derrin and Chloe were entertaining guests at an engagement party hosted by his parents. The courtyard was decorated with yellow, red and white roses surrounding the tables, walkway and candles. Chloe was dressed in a lovely emerald sequin dress, specifically selected to coordinate with her engagement ring. Kenya gladly helped in the selection by dragging Chloe to every boutique, mall and shopping center in the ten county area. Chloe chuckled, she did not complain. She loved every minute of it.

Chloe was discussing the invitation colors with Kenya, Cara and Diane. While, Derrin was sitting at a linen covered table laughing with his friends, Jared, Ennis, Calvin and Marcus. Marcus was recounting the night when Derrin chased Chloe to the hotel. He explained the bet he and his fellow officers made. "Dee, I need you to have Chloe reveal the winner of my bet. The guys at the station have a pool going on over who actually won the bet. Of course, I think I won because I said you would beg Chloe to take you back. Officer Tony claims he won because you did not beg her in the lobby."

Calvin interjected and said, "I thought you told me the old lady gave you a copy of the hotel video showing the whole thing." Marcus kicked Calvin under the table.

"What?" Calvin blurted.

"Derrin, man I need you to tell us if you got down on your knees and begged Chloe. The camera didn't catch everything. Even if you didn't beg can you just say you did, so I can win the bet?" Derrin grinned.

"What happened behind closed doors is between me and Chloe. And I'm not telling."

Marcus finally turned to Derrin, "So you keeping secrets, alright then." All the friends continued ribbing each other. Until Derrin's face turned serious.

"Secrets? Look who's talking. The biggest secret keeper here." Derrin replied directing his comment to Marcus.

"Man, I have no clue what you're talking about." Marcus sincerely appeared bewildered by the accusation.

"Don't act. You know what I'm talking about. You think I don't know about you and my sister. Not even you, a law enforcement officer can keep things from me."

Marcus was dumbfounded. He did not plan to have this conversation until he was certain Derrin was thousands of miles away on a honeymoon. As he sat there deep in thought, Jared pulled Calvin and Ennis away to an area populated by single women. Jared wanted to give Derrin privacy to have this discussion.

"What are your intentions for my sister?"

Derrin's words brought Marcus out of his thoughts. He cleared his throat and sipped his drink. He met Derrin's gaze and did not blink.

"I intend to make her love me as much as I love her. I intend to make her my wife and the mother of my children. I intend to make her happy for the rest of her life."

Derrin patted Marcus on the back and smiled. "Does Kenya know your plan?" Marcus shook his head and did not say a word. Derrin nearly choked on his drink before he replied. "It looks like you have a death sentence. Good luck on that." Marcus was relieved this was the sum total of the entire discussion about Kenya.

Derrin spotted Chloe walking his way and decided he had better things to do than sitting around talking about his sister's relationship. He reached Chloe and he whispered in her ear all the plans he had for her later.

CPSIA information can be obtained at www.ICGtesting.com
Printed in the USA
LVOW092043181211

260031LV00001B/168/P